The Summer of May

Cecilia Galante

Aladdin

New York London Toronto Sydney New Delhi

ALADDIN
An imprint of Simon & Schuster Children's Publishing Division
1230 Avenue of the Americas, New York, NY 10020
First Aladdin paperback edition April 2012

For information about special discounts for bulk purchases, please contact Simon & Schuster Special Sales at 1-866-506-1949 or business@simonandschuster.com.
The Simon & Schuster Speakers Bureau can bring authors to your live event. For more information or to book an event contact the Simon & Schuster Speakers Bureau at 1-866-248-3049 or visit our website at www.simonspeakers.com.
Designed by Jessica Handelman
The text of this book was set in Fairfield LH.
Manufactured in the United States of America 0312 OFF
2 4 6 8 10 9 7 5 3 1
The Library of Congress has cataloged the hardcover edition as follows:
Galante, Cecilia.
The summer of May / by Cecilia Galante — 1st Aladdin hardcover ed.
p. cm.
Summary: An angry thirteen-year-old girl and her hated English teacher spend a summer school class together, learning surprising things about each other.
ISBN 978-1-4169-8023-0 (hc)
[1. Teachers—Fiction. 2. Anger—Fiction. 3. Loss (Psychology)—Fiction. 4. Mothers and daughters—Fiction. 5. Summer—Fiction.] I. Title.
PZ7.G12965Su 2011 [Fic]—dc22 2010015879
ISBN 978-1-4169-8304-0 (pbk)
ISBN 978-1-4169-8590-7 (eBook)

For my father, a man among men.
And the best storyteller I know.

Acknowledgments

First, thanks goes to my agent, Jessica Regel, who continues to champion my work as well as assuage any and all doubts on my part. (Not an easy feat.) There's no one else in the business like you, Jess. I count my blessings every day.

Thank you also to the lovely Kate Angelella, editor extraordinaire, who showed me another side to May I hadn't realized was there—making for a richer, more poignant story overall. Everyone at Simon & Schuster who worked tirelessly on this book deserves a special shout-out. I am indebted to all of you for standing behind me and contributing such fantastic work.

My family and friends are the ones who, in the end, make all this possible. Thank you to my husband, Paul, King of Bathtime, Bedtime Stories, and Earwax Removal, for taking over when I can't be there; my children, Sarah, Sophia, and Joseph, who not only encourage me to keep writing but sometimes push me out the door so they can stay up late with aforementioned King; and my friends, especially Kemi, Rachel, Don, Gina, and Mollie, for cheering along the way. (And for sharing the wine when the work is over.)

Finally, I would like to thank the very first eighth-grade class I ever taught at E. L. Meyers High School. I had each and every one of them in mind as I wrote this story, since all of them, by year's end, had created an indelible mark on me.

I'll never forget you guys.

1

I thought it was funny.

So did a lot of other kids.

Miss Movado, however, did not.

Neither did Principal Mola, the middle school principal. Principal Mola used to be a drill sergeant in the army. With his shaved head and starched shirts, he still looks like one. He glared at me now above his steepled fingers, waiting, I guess, for me to burst into tears and admit that I was responsible. Instead I stared at the mounted fish that hung on the wall behind his head. Its silvery scales had been painted a dark blue on the bottom and a nose, sharp as a needle, stuck out of the front of it. I wondered if deep down, Principal Mola wished he could do the same thing to some of his students that he'd done to that fish.

"Maeve," Principal Mola said sternly. "Look at me."

I bristled. "It's *May*. Not Maeve."

"May." Principal Mola stood up, leaning his whole weight on just the tips of his fingers until they turned white. "Look at me." I glanced over at him. A tiny bead of sweat was balanced on his upper lip. "We know it was you. Pete *saw* you in her room with the spray-paint can."

Pete was the school janitor. I'd seen the top of his bald head go by through the little square hole in Miss Movado's door just as I was finishing up, and jumped so fast into the coat closet that I almost fell over. It was a tiny, airless space. One of Miss Movado's hideous cardigan sweaters was hanging behind me. I waited, inhaling the scent of butterscotch and her too-sweet perfume, until I thought I might get sick. Ten minutes went by, but Pete did not return. Finally I slipped back out, grabbed the can of spray paint, and ran. It hadn't even occurred to me that he might have seen me.

I shifted in my chair. The back of my legs made a peeling sound against the red leather. "Pete couldn't have seen me," I said. "Because I wasn't *there*."

Principal Mola studied me for a moment, as if examining a new specimen of fish. How long had that poor fish struggled? I wondered, glancing up at it once more. How hard had Principal Mola pulled and reeled his line until, exhausted, the poor thing had given up? Probably pretty long. Well, he wasn't going to reel *me* in, no matter how hard he pulled or how long he tried.

"We have *video* of you in the hallway too, Maeve. Right outside Miss Movado's classroom. Just you. No one else."

My cheeks flushed hot. I'd forgotten about the school cameras. "It must've been someone else. Someone who looks like me."

Principal Mola shook his head as he came around to the front of his desk. Leaning back against the smooth wood, he crossed his arms over his red tie. A gold wedding ring peeked out from the finger on his left hand. "You're thirteen years old now, May, correct?" I didn't answer. He knew how old I was. "Where along the line do you think you picked up such a blatant disrespect for authority?"

This was the eighth time this year that I'd been in Principal Mola's office. The last time was because I was involved in a food fight in the cafeteria. It hadn't been a big one—just a few Tater Tots hurled across the room at Jeremy Finkster, who'd thrown one at me first. Maybe a chocolate pudding, too. But Principal Mola had gone off on the whole disrespect for authority spiel during that visit too. It was his army thing. His "Give me five minutes, and I'll crush you like a bug" routine. I stared at the blue swirl pattern in the rug and jiggled my leg up and down.

"Do you have any idea where this attitude of yours is going to take you?" Principal Mola decided to try a different tactic. "Any idea at all? I'll tell you. Nowhere, young lady. Actually, I stand corrected. It *is* going to take you somewhere. It's going to take you to one big dead end. Period."

The swirls in the rug were actually a whole bunch of large and small paisley shapes, all crammed together. If I turned my head just a little to the right, they almost looked like they were moving. A great big sea of blue paisleys. Kind of cool.

Principal Mola pulled the cuff of his right shirt sleeve down over his wrist, and then the other. He picked a piece of lint off the front of his creased pants and tossed it in the trash can next to him. "Listen, I know you've had a tough year, Maeve. With everything that happened to your—"

"It's *May*!" It came out louder than I expected, more to drown out the rest of Principal Mola's sentence than to correct my name. Something tightened in the back of my throat, a pinpoint of pain, and I swallowed over it. "Could you pleaseplease*please* just call me May? Please. I hate the name Maeve."

Principal Mola rolled his bottom lip over his teeth. "Let's get to the real point of this meeting, shall we? I'm here to inform you that Miss Movado has agreed not to press charges."

"Wait, what?" My foot stopped jiggling. A flash of heat spread out along my arms, all the way up to the back of my neck. "*Charges?* What kind of charges?"

"Defacing school property. Using foul and derogatory language in regard to a teacher."

"But I didn't *do* it!" I got up out of my chair, fists clenched at my side.

"You *did* do it." Principal Mola's voice was so sharp and so final that for a moment, I almost wavered. Almost. "*I* know you did it, and *you* know you did it. And we are not going to waste any more time going back and forth about it. You have two options. You can either be expelled—"

"Expelled?" I repeated. "I thought you just said Miss Movado wasn't going to press charges."

"She's isn't," Principal Mola answered coolly. "But I still can."

I sat back down again.

Principal Mola nodded. "I'm assuming you don't want to go that route."

I stared stoically at the rug. Shook my head the merest bit.

"All right, then. These are your options: You can agree to expulsion from this school, *or* you can retake eighth-grade English with Miss Movado in summer school."

"Retake *English*?" I gripped the sides of the chair. "But

I don't need to retake English! I didn't fail it!"

"That's not what Miss Movado seems to think." Principal Mola turned slightly to the right, pressed a button on his phone, and then spoke into it. "All right, Lucille. Send Miss Movado in, please."

I swiveled around in my chair as the door opened. With her tiny head, wide hips, and stubby legs, it was not hard to imagine where the nickname Movado the Avocado had come from. It didn't help that her favorite color was green, either. The shirt she had on now was the same shade as celery, and her pants—a polyester blend that made a swiffing sound when she walked—were the color of limes. But Miss Movado's sad appearance belied her personality. She was the most feared—and hated—teacher in the whole school. She came down on students with a hurricane force. In her classroom, Movado the Avocado made Principal Mola look like Bo Peep. I couldn't imagine having to spend another *period* with her—let alone an entire summer. It would be the equivalent of torture.

Miss Movado gave Principal Mola a curt nod and sat down in the chair next to me.

"You failed me?" I stared at Movado the Avocado. "That is not fair! Is this, like, some kind of revenge?"

Movado the Avocado did not answer me. She stared straight ahead at the wall and blinked once.

"What would she need to get revenge for?" Principal Mola asked carefully.

"For . . ." I stumbled, trying to get my thoughts in order. "For not liking English or something, I guess!" Even I knew it sounded stupid, but it was all I could think of.

"This has nothing to do with not liking English." Movado the Avocado was still staring at the wall. "My job is not to get you to *like* English." Her voice was tight, but strangely soft. I leaned back in my chair a little. It was the first time I'd heard her talk in a normal tone of voice. Usually she was pacing around the classroom, roaring and yelling like some kind of deranged dinosaur.

"Then what'd you fail me for?"

Movado the Avocado turned her head so that she was looking directly at me. Her wide face was damp with perspiration. Small black hairs quivered along her upper lip, and a single curl clung like seaweed against her forehead. "To try again," she said. "The right way."

"To try *what* again?" I asked.

"All of it," Movado the Avocado said. "Technically, you did pass my class, May. By one point. The effort you put into the work I gave you all year was minimal at best, nonexistent at worst. I want you to do it again—with effort this time—the way you should have done it in the first place." Her voice was unnervingly quiet. It creeped me out.

"You can't *force* people to do things, you know." I sat back and crossed my arms. "This is America. Land of the free, in case you haven't noticed."

"Oh, I've noticed," Movado the Avocado answered. "And you're perfectly free to choose whatever option Principal Mola just presented to you. Me or expulsion." She shrugged. "You'll just have to find another school to go to next year."

I glared at her. Narrowed my eyes at Principal Mola.

But no matter how hard I looked at both of them, the only thing I could see was the wide white sail of my eighth-grade summer slipping away.

2

"What'd he say?" Olive asked as I walked back into the cafeteria. She tapped the empty space where she'd saved a seat for me at the end of the table. Around us, the rest of the student body hummed with excitement. It was the last day of school. In less than an hour, we were going to be dismissed for the last time. Everyone would run for the front doors, screaming with anticipation of the summer that loomed ahead.

Everyone but me.

I sat down, glancing at the table across the room where Brittany Martinson and her crew were huddled over a Victoria's Secret catalog. For some reason, whenever they turned a page, the sounds of shrieking and laughing burst out from the middle of the group. Ugh. Sometimes I still couldn't believe that Olive and I used to hang out with them. It was probably just because we'd all shared the same homeroom for two years. Now, though, at the end of our eighth-grade year, I barely recognized them anymore. Especially Brittany. She'd practically turned into an alien with all the makeup she wore, and the weird way she did her hair. I mean, she barely even looked *human* anymore.

Of course, they probably all thought the same thing about me, which is why none of us talked anymore. I didn't used to have the temper I had now. And I guess all my outbursts over the last year kind of scared them off. A few months ago, there'd been one final incident between us that ended things for good. It had started out just between Brittany and me, and ended up with all four of them screaming in my face. (Olive had stood off to one side, just watching.) They all hated me now. And my temper. Olive was the only one who'd stuck around.

I crossed my arms and put my head down.

"Was it that bad?" Olive asked.

I held up a finger, which was my "I need a minute" sign.

"Okay." I could hear Olive's feet sliding across the floor. "Just tell me when you're ready."

Olive wore very sensible clothes and no makeup. She pinned her long brown hair back on either side with tortoiseshell barrettes, and wore the same pair of red ladybug earrings every day. Some people classified her as a nerd because she was smart and kept mostly to herself, but I didn't think of her that way. I just thought she was different—which I liked. She had what Momma used to call a "duck temperament." Everything rolled off her back. It was an attitude I was pretty sure she got from her own mother, who was employed as something called a life coach. People came and talked to Olive's mom about their lives falling apart, and she helped them get back on track. Sometimes Olive could be full of good advice too.

"May?" Olive's soft voice drifted over the table. "You okay?"

I lifted my head. "She's making me go to summer school."

"Who is?"

"Movado the Avocado."

"Why? You didn't fail English."

"That's what I said."

"Then why?" Olive asked.

"Revenge, I guess. For what I did to her room."

"Did you *tell* them it was you?" Olive's gray eyes went wide.

I shook my head. "I didn't have to. They have me on video in the hallway. Plus Pete saw me."

Olive pursed her lips. She arched her left eyebrow and gave me one of her "I told you so" looks. She'd been the one who had tried to talk me down after I had gotten the idea in my head and told her what I was going to do. "Revenge is stupid," she'd said. "Seriously, May. The best revenge is forgiveness." Every so often, Olive liked to use her mother's life coach quotes on me. I didn't mind the advice she gave me sometimes, but the quotes drove me nuts.

"Forgiveness?" I sputtered. "Are you kidding me? I wouldn't forgive that woman if you paid me a million bucks! She embarrassed me in front of the whole class! She made me feel like a total idiot!" Olive stared at me with the sad little expression she sometimes used when she knew she hadn't gotten through to me, but I didn't care. All I knew was that I'd wanted to humiliate Miss Movado the way she had humiliated me.

"So even though you didn't technically fail her class, Movado's making you take it over?" Olive asked. "Like, just for punishment?"

I nodded. "It was that or get expelled."

Olive leaned forward. "They were going to *expel* you?"

I let my head sink back down against the table again. "All our summer plans," I groaned. "Down the tube."

Actually, we hadn't had much planned. There was the public pool, where we'd go when it got too hot to do anything else. We'd probably rent movies at Olive's house, which had air-conditioning, or hang out at the Rite Aid on Fridays so we could leaf through all the new celebrity magazines and buy junk food. Olive had been bugging me to go with her to the mall, too, so she could pick out a pair of Doc Martens like the ones I wore every day. Mine were black and stopped at the ankle. Olive wanted a bright blue pair that laced up around her calves. But she didn't want to go get them by herself. She was nervous about it for some reason, as if once the salesperson took a look at her, he might laugh out loud when she told him what she wanted. I told her I'd go with her.

"Well, it's only half a day," Olive pointed out. "Summer school, I mean. We'll still have time to hang out. Maybe you could even take me up to Hot Topic." She was talking about the Doc Martens again.

"I guess."

"What do you think your dad's going to say?"

The two of us locked eyes for a moment. Olive had seen more sides of my dad than I wished she had. The last time she had come over, Dad and I got into a really loud argument. I mean, *really* loud. Olive slipped out before I even noticed she was gone. She rarely came over to my place at all anymore. Olive didn't like noisy people.

"Principal Mola already told him," I said. "He was

supposed to come down for the meeting just now, but he couldn't make it."

Olive's forehead creased. "Work?"

"I guess. What else? Whatever. I'll deal with it."

"What about your gram?" Olive asked. "You even gonna tell her?"

I'd been trying not to think about Gram all day. Now her face flooded the inside of my head. Her white hair and soft, papery skin. Big blue eyes that spent more time wet than dry. I knew she missed Momma just as much as I did—maybe even more. In the year and a half that Momma had left, Gram had turned into a whole other person. She'd lost so much weight since Christmas that she was nearly half her size. Her once chubby-cheeked face had become pale and drawn, and she looked too small now inside her bathrobe.

She acted differently too. Gram used to be a real smart aleck. She was funny and sarcastic and no matter how bad of a mood I was in, she could get me laughing in about two minutes flat. Now, when she overcooked the chicken one night for dinner, she cried for so long that I thought she would never stop. And she had stopped interfering whenever Dad and I argued, which these days was an almost daily occurrence. It used to be that no matter what the situation was, she took my side. Now when our voices escalated, she just went into her room and shut the door.

"I don't think I should tell her," I said. "I mean, what's the point?"

Olive nodded. "I agree. Your gram's got enough on her plate right now."

At the other end of the table, Nikki Reiser stood up. She was part of Brittany's crew, and the prettiest girl in the school. "You are *so* not a B cup, Ashley!" she said, her hand on her hip. "Don't even *try*!" Ashley's face turned a pale fuchsia color. She yanked Nikki back down in her seat. Next to them, Brittany laughed and clapped her hands.

I looked back at Olive. Rolled my eyes.

"You want to do something after school?" Olive asked.

"I gotta go check on Gram."

"I know." Olive reached up and turned her ladybug earring. "I meant after."

"Rite Aid?" I asked. "Three thirty?"

Olive grinned. "I'll be there."

3

You would have thought someone was giving away free concert tickets the way everyone barreled out the front door when that last bell rang. It was like a stampede or something, with kids shoving and screaming and trying to get past all the teachers without knocking one of them over. Someone even threw a book bag up in the air, which made a whole bunch of girls scream, and then Brian Bunker slid down the black banister along the steps and fell at the bottom of it, which made them scream even louder.

Not me. What did I have to yell or run about? My summer was going to be a disaster. And so after I said good-bye to Olive (who lived in the opposite direction), I just walked home at my regular steady pace, the way I always did.

Sometimes, when I walked, I counted all the Volkswagen Bugs, but I was too down in the dumps today to do that, so I just kept my head down and kept going.

I didn't even have to raise my head to know when I'd turned onto Ransom Street, because there were so many plastic soda bottles and Burger King bags littering the edges of the sidewalk that it looked as if a garbage truck had opened the back of the truck and let everything slide out. The middle of the street was littered with deep, jagged potholes, and the houses had been built so close together that if you stood between them and stretched out your arms, you could touch both sides.

But the worst thing about living on Ransom Street was the noise.

At any given moment, someone was either yelling, or playing basketball, or revving up a car engine. Friday and Saturday nights were the worst, after people came back late from the bars. Then, anything could happen. I actually saw a chair fly out of a second-story window once, after some lady started hollering. There was broken glass everywhere; in the distance, you could hear a baby crying. The police were here for the rest of the night, their lights making red and blue shadows throughout my room while I tried to get back to sleep.

When Momma was still around, we'd lived in an

apartment on a really nice street, just a few miles away. It was half of a whole house, and it had an upstairs and a downstairs. We'd even had a backyard—with two trees!—and everyone else in the neighborhood kept their places as nice-looking as Momma kept ours. After she left, though, we'd had to move to Ransom Street. Dad couldn't afford the nice apartment anymore on his own, and, he said, that was just the way it was. We had to make do.

Now I looked out of the corner of my eye as I made my way down the street toward my building. Two high school guys were sitting on the front steps of a house across from mine, smoking cigarettes. The steps were split at the end; peels of paint curled off the sides. A few houses down, three older men were standing around the hood of a car, peering inside. Two of them were drinking beer. None of them were wearing shirts. Gross.

I opened the metal door on the side of the house that led up to our apartment. Fingers of heat wrapped themselves around me as I went up the steps, squeezing more and more tightly until, as I reached the door, they felt as if they were closing off my throat completely. I pushed open the door and inhaled. "Gram?"

No answer.

But she never answered anymore. I threw my book bag on the tiny kitchen table and walked across the living room. Our old house was so spacious that when I was little, I used to be able to ride my Big Wheel tricycle through the living room, down the hallway, into the kitchen, and back around again. Now, in the span of about ten short steps, I could move from the kitchen, to the living room, and into Gram's bedroom. We didn't even have a hallway.

I knocked lightly on her door, but didn't push it open. "Gram?"

"Hi, honey." Her voice sounded drowsy, as if I had just wakened her.

"Are you okay?" I lowered my voice a little. "Do you need anything?"

"Just taking a nap," Gram said. "I don't need a thing."

"I'm going out for a little bit with Olive. I'll be back in an hour or so, all right?"

"Fine, dear."

I ducked into my room (which was right next to Gram's) to check on Sherman. Sherman was my hermit crab. I'd had him for three years. Some people thought that hermit crabs weren't "real" pets, because they couldn't go on walks or snuggle up with you in bed, but Sherman was one of the best pets I'd ever had. He had a personality like you wouldn't believe, and last year I taught him how to stand on his head. Now, though, he was asleep. He must've been taking cues from Gram.

I stopped in the bathroom before I left, just so I could brush my teeth. I brushed my teeth about six or seven times a day, or whenever I felt that slick, gritty layer starting to accumulate along the edges. I even kept a toothbrush in my backpack so that I could brush after lunch. I glanced in the mirror as I brushed, and then winced, the way I always did whenever I saw my reflection. From far away, I probably just came across as a small, skinny girl with big feet. Up close, though, it looked as if I'd wandered into a freckle factory—and it had exploded. Behind the freckles were a pair of light green eyes, a small nose, and crooked teeth.

Horrible. And then some.

But Olive was waiting. And I wasn't the kind of girl to stand around and cry because I didn't look like a supermodel.

Instead I rinsed, spit, and wiped my mouth.

Time to go.

4

The inside of Rite Aid was air-conditioned, which was a welcome relief from the heat. The blue carpeting on the floor almost looked like water, and just inside the doors against the wall, someone had arranged at least fifty tins of powdered lemonade mix into a towering pyramid. Summer had officially arrived.

Olive was already over in the magazine section, which was where we always planted ourselves when we came to the store on Fridays. We'd been reprimanded once for standing there and eating potato chips while we read (the manager said we were "soiling" the magazine pages), but he didn't seem to mind if we looked at them and bought our snacks later.

"Anything good?" I peered over Olive's shoulder, staring

down at a glossy picture of a girl and a guy dressed in bathing suits. They were holding hands and walking along a beach. The girl was wearing a bikini, of course, while he was dressed in big, baggy shorts that came down to his knees. Neither of them had shoes on. Above them, in large letters, was the headline: SECRET ROMANCE!

"Anything *good*?" Olive held the magazine out at arm's length, as if letting the picture speak for itself. "Look!"

I leaned in a little closer. "Wasn't he on *American Idol*?"

"Yes!" Olive stared at me. "So what the heck is she *doing* with him?"

I shrugged. "Come on, let's do something else."

Olive's eyes widened. "But they're all new today!" She swept the arrangement of celebrity magazines with a wave of her hand. "I gotta see what's going on!"

Most of the time, I didn't mind looking at the magazines either. It was fun to see which star was hooking up with what singer, and who had put on eighty-five pounds overnight. But Olive lived for this stuff. She could stand around all day, just reading all these goofy stories. Her mother wouldn't let her read the magazines at home, which was why she couldn't buy a subscription to them, and neither of us really had any money anyway, which was why we read them in the store. But today I didn't feel like looking at any of them, much less reading the stories.

"I'm going over to the vitamin aisle," I said. "Come over when you're ready." I drifted up and down the aisle for a while, pausing every few minutes or so to pick up a box of something, which I pretended to read. Vitamin E, apparently, could help heal scars. And there was something in a jar called fish oil caplets, which were supposed to keep your hair shiny. Gross.

I kept wandering back to the end of the aisle and glancing over at Olive, waiting for her to come join me. But she was completely immersed in that magazine. I mean, nothing was budging her. Next to the vitamin aisle were the greeting card shelves. I looked through a few aimlessly: There were a ton of graduation ones, a bunch of birthday greetings, even one that said "For Your First Tooth." And then all the way on the left, next to the one about the tooth, I saw it.

A whole row of leftover Mother's Day cards. They were all pink, of course, which made my face get hot right away, because people who make cards think that all girls and mothers always love the color pink, when in fact they don't. And they were the corniest things I had ever seen, with fake-looking photographs of brown and yellow flowers on the front, surrounded by all these gold curlicues and happy, bouncy ribbons. The poems inside were even worse. Stuff like: "No one's ever loved me like you," and "When I'm with you, Mother, my world is complete." I mean, things that make you want to gag.

So I was just standing there, with my face getting hotter and hotter, reading this stupid, putrid stuff, and I was just about ready to put back the card I was holding, although I hadn't quite gotten around to it yet, when Olive came bounding up.

"Hey." She slowed when she saw the card in my hand. (It was the one about my world being complete.) "What're you doing?"

I put the card back in the sleeve. "Nothing."

Olive was looking at me, though, with that worried expression of hers. She touched me along the wrist as I started walking. "May? Are you okay?"

"Of course I'm okay." I swallowed and lifted my hair off the back of my neck, where little beads of sweat had started to form. "C'mon, let's go look at the snacks."

We stood in front of the snack aisle for a few minutes. I was pretending to deliberate—Doritos? Chex Mix? Salted almonds?—but nothing was registering. I wasn't even hungry. That always happened, though, when I came across something that made me think of Momma. Even if it was an ugly leftover Mother's Day card.

We settled finally on a bag of chocolate pretzels and a bottle of water, and shared them outside on a bench behind the store. The heat rose in a shimmer across the street, making the sides of the cars look blurred, and there was no breeze. Olive and I did not talk, which made me feel grateful and worried at the same time.

Finally, though, as we were finishing off the last of the pretzels, Olive turned and poked me in the arm. "It's over," she said.

I stared at her. "What?"

"School," she said. "It's over. Can you believe it?"

My breath, which had started to speed up, began to slow back down again. "Yeah." I swallowed the last of the water and then wiped my lips with the back of my hand. "Well, maybe for some of us."

5

Later that evening, waiting for Dad to come home with dinner, I found myself thinking about those cards again. For some reason, I couldn't remember what the Mother's Day card I'd bought for Momma just before she left looked like. I'd bought it from a store; that much I knew. The last time I'd made her a card was when I was about eight years old. Back then, I made cards for her all the time—even if it wasn't Mother's Day—drawing the word "Mom" in big, puffy letters and coloring them in with my crayons. Sometimes I'd add bumblebees and butterflies, just to make it pretty. Once I even drew her a giant panda bear holding a heart. But the last Mother's Day card had been from the store. Why couldn't I remember what it said? Or even what it looked like?

I tried to distract myself by playing with Sherman, and checking my MySpace page. But no one was on MySpace, and Sherman didn't want to play. He kept sticking out his claws and pinching me whenever I tried to pick him up. So I put him back in his cage and picked up the harmonica Dad had given me two Christmases ago. It was a real silver harmonica—a Lee Oskar ten-hole diatonic—that actual musicians used. Dad had one too. With red trim on the side and a double pipe, it was a nice-looking instrument. And it had a real weight to it, not like one of those cheap plastic ones you could get sometimes out of a gumball machine.

Dad had shown me the basics, like how to hold it and the notes and all that, but the only song he'd gotten around to teaching me before Momma left was an old one from the 1960s called "Moon River." Nothing since. He hadn't touched his own harmonica in over a year, and I never played it when he was home anymore.

But I loved "Moon River." I didn't know the words, but the music was sad and happy and hopeful and depressing all at the same time. Now, I played "Moon River" all the way through three times, and then sat very still, the way I always did when I blew the last note. Sometimes, afterward, it felt as if I had gone inside a bubble, as if the notes themselves had formed something around me that nothing else could touch.

Except maybe the heat. The temperature in our apartment was at least eighty-five degrees—even with the windows open. My room felt like a steam cloud. Dad had fans parked all over the place, but all they did was blow the hot air around the rooms. My stomach growled again too. I didn't know what was taking Dad so long, but I got up and went into the kitchen to find something to eat. I paused outside of Gram's door, which was slightly ajar, and peeked in. She was sitting on her bed, her legs stuck out straight underneath her pale blue sheets, staring at the wall. A game of solitaire had been laid out neatly on the space of sheet next to her, and the tiny lamp behind her bed had been turned on.

"Gram?" I pushed open the door a little. Her room smelled like Vicks VapoRub.

She looked up, startled, and then patted the sheet next to her. "May. Come sit with me."

I walked over, dread filling my chest like water, and sat down on the edge of her bed. Whenever Gram invited me into her room, it was because she wanted to tell me some kind of story. Usually about Momma. And I didn't want to hear it.

She took my hand in hers. "Did I ever tell you about the time your momma ran away to join the circus when she was a little girl?" Her eyes were bright, but her mouth trembled as she spoke.

"No," I said. "Tell me."

Gram patted my hand. The collar of her lilac housecoat was turned under on one side. "Well. She was no more than eight years old. And she had a little friend in the neighborhood. A girl named Violet. They did everything together. Everything! I'd come into your mother's room on Saturday mornings and find the two of them fast asleep in the same bed. I didn't even know Violet had spent the night!"

The merest smile passed over Gram's face, remembering.

"Anyway, one day the circus came to town. The grade school took your mother's class to see it, but she came home that same afternoon and insisted that we all go that night, too. She said she would not be able to *live* if she could not see the trapeze artists fly through the air again. So we went. We took Violet, of course. We took Violet everywhere." Gram paused for a moment, frowning a little. "If I remember correctly, Violet did not have the best home life." Another pause. "Anyway, we got popcorn and cotton candy and sat in the very top row of the stands so we could get the best view. When the trapeze artists came out and did their thing, Violet and your mother held hands the whole time. And I remember . . ."

Gram paused, her eyes looking out at something I

couldn't see. For a moment, I held my breath, wondering if she was going to cry. She cried a lot. She didn't care anymore.

"I remember looking over at her—at your mother—at one point and being amazed at the expression on her face. I'd never seen anything like it. She was just . . . oh, I'm not good with words . . . just so . . . *happy*, May. So full of joy. It was like looking at someone who had just seen heaven. Like she was lit from the inside out."

I studied the folds of Gram's quilt. I'd never seen Momma's face look like that. Not once. Not ever.

"Do you think she wanted to be a trapeze artist?" I asked.

Gram looked at me. "I think she wanted to fly," she said softly. She held my gaze for a moment and then looked away. "Anyway, the next morning the two of them were gone. Violet and your mother. They were very thoughtful about it; they left a note on the kitchen table that said that they were running away to join the circus and that they would send us all the money they earned as acrobats. I found them down on the circus grounds, chatting up the ringmaster, who was trying to arrange for them to get back home. It took a little convincing—and an acrobatic lesson from one of the trapeze ladies—to get them to come back with me, but they did." Gram sighed. "They did."

It was a nice story, I guessed, but like all of Gram's stories about Momma, it ended too abruptly. I rubbed her hand softly. "Listen, are you hungry?"

Gram reached over and picked up a six of spades. "No."

"Did you have lunch?"

"Soup," she said. "And some raisins."

"I'm going to make myself a grilled cheese. And I'm going to make you one too. You have to eat it, Gram. Okay?"

She nodded.

"Gram."

"Yes, May. I'll eat it, honey."

I left the room.

We both knew she wouldn't.

6

I went back out to the kitchen and grabbed the loaf of white bread out of the bread box. The refrigerator contents were getting low: a half gallon of water, six individually wrapped slices of cheese, a quart of milk, fried chicken leftovers, and a mound of congealed spaghetti in a plastic bowl. I grabbed the cheese, put a flame under a frying pan, and dropped a chunk of butter in the middle of it. It skittered and sizzled across the metal surface, a fat yellow water bug.

Behind me, the door opened.

"Hey, Dad." I glanced over my shoulder, hoping my voice sounded casual. "Did you bring dinner?"

He hung his baseball hat on the hook near the door. "No. Was I supposed to?"

I turned back to the stove. "You said you would this morning."

"I'm sorry." Dad unbuckled his tool belt and dropped it on the floor. It landed with a thud. Any minute now we would hear Mr. Reynolds, who lived downstairs, start banging on the ceiling with his broom handle, which is what he always did when things got too loud up here.

"It's all right." I tilted the pan, letting the butter coat the sides. "I'm making grilled cheeses."

A faint cloud of dust rose up around Dad as he collapsed on the couch. He worked on the highways, building roads, repairing potholes, laying down hot gravel and pressing it flat into the ground. His skin and clothing were always covered with dust. He lifted his feet and unlaced his heavy boots, kicking them off. Clunk. Clunk.

Our apartment had only two bedrooms, so Dad slept on the couch and kept all his stuff in the hall closet. During the day, when he was gone at work, the apartment actually felt a little spacious. But when he got home, the walls started closing in again. Sometimes, if I got up in the middle of the night to go to the bathroom, I'd fall over one his boots. On Thanksgiving night last year, I tripped over his tool belt and had to get six stitches in my knee.

I laid a piece of bread down in the pan and counted to

ten. Next came the cheese—two slices—and the second piece of buttered bread.

Dad walked into the kitchen. He opened the refrigerator and stood there, staring into it. He smelled like tar and cigarettes. "You gonna tell me what happened today?" he asked. "Or do I have to guess?"

I closed my eyes. Took a deep breath. "I have to go to summer school."

Dad took out the jug of water and closed the refrigerator. He drank in great gulps, his Adam's apple rising and falling inside his throat. Then he wiped his mouth with the back of his hand. "Summer school?"

I pressed the spatula against the top of the sandwich. "It was that or get expelled."

"*Darn* it, May!" He slammed the jug down on the counter. "What the heck were you thinking?"

I cringed inwardly and flipped the sandwich, inhaling the scent of cheese and butter.

"These people aren't gonna keep letting you off the hook, you know." He opened the refrigerator again and threw the jug back in. "You keep this crap up and one of these days, you're gonna push them too far. You'll end up sitting by yourself in some little room in juvenile detention, crying your eyes out."

I spun around. "I will not!"

"You will!" Dad yelled. "And I'll tell you something else! *I'm* not gonna be around to come pick you up when it happens! Next time, you're gonna have to do it on your own!"

"Pick me up?" I repeated. "You? Pick me up? For what? You've never picked me up for anything!"

"Don't start with me." Dad pointed his index finger in my face. I hated it when he did that. One time I slapped it away, and he caught me around the wrist. His face was so furious and his grip so tight that I never did it again. "You have no idea how many times I've gotten you out of your messes, May. None. So don't you start with that flippy little attitude of yours, or you're going to find out what it's like to have to figure things out on your own."

I leaned back, away from his finger, and bumped into the frying pan. The acrid smell of cheese burning wafted up behind me. "Look what you did!" Furious, I turned around, flicked off the heat, and shoved the frying pan across the stove. "You made me burn my sandwich! That was my dinner! And Gram's, too!"

"Make another one," Dad said, walking into the living room. His voice was tired. "And stop yelling."

"I'll yell all I want! I don't care!"

Beneath us came three rapid knocks from Mr. Reynolds's broom handle.

Dad grabbed one of his boots and pounded it three times on the floor, right where the broom handle had sounded. Then he strode back across the living room and into the kitchen. He stuck his finger in my face again. "You'd better *start* caring," he said. "Because if you don't, you're gonna end up alone and miserable. Just like your mother."

The weight of his words staggered me. I had to actually reach out and hold on to the side of the counter, because I thought I might fall down. "I hate you!" I screamed. "I hate you! I hate you! I hate you!"

Downstairs, the broom handle pounded again. Six raps this time.

Dad stomped his foot six times on the floor.

I ran into my room.

Gram's door was already shut.

7

I HATE HIS GUTS, I texted Olive. HE'S SUCH A JERK.

I looked out at the street from my perch inside my bedroom window. It was almost dark, but the air was still hot and thick. Two little boys were playing basketball a little way down, in front of someone's driveway. I didn't see any net, but that didn't seem to bother either of them; they dribbled and threw and shot the ball in wide arcs, as if the net was just invisible. The sound of a baby crying floated out from a house a few doors down, followed by the slamming of a door. A woman's voice yelled something rude.

R U GROUNDED? Olive texted back.

NO.

THAT'S GOOD.

A red car drifted down the street, slowly, as if the driver was looking for someone. A thin white streak had been painted down the side, exploding into a small shape of flame toward the back, and the radio had been turned to a ridiculous volume. Music pounded the insides of the car like a rubber bat. It stopped next to the boys, who broke from their basketball game. The driver, who had a black bandanna over his head, leaned out the window. He turned the music down as they started talking.

MAY? In my hand, my phone buzzed. THAT'S GOOD, RIGHT?

I GUESS.

WHAT HAPPENED?

HE SAID NEXT TIME I WOULD END UP IN JUVIE & HE WOULDN'T COME GET ME.

OUCH.

The driver in the red car was still talking to the boys. It sounded like his voice was getting louder. Suddenly one of them pushed his way to the front and shoved his head into the car window. I could hear words being yelled, but I couldn't tell who was saying what. The other boy pulled on his friend's arm. He looked alarmed, frightened even. Without warning, the red car gunned its engine. With a screech of tires, it peeled off down the street, narrowly missing Dad's truck, which was parked in front of our building.

SO R U OK? Olive texted.

I HATE IT HERE.

IT'S NOT SO BAD.

YOU DON'T LIVE ON RANSOM STREET. It was true. Olive lived on Vine Street, six blocks over from me. It was amazing how in the span of so short a distance, houses and sidewalks and front lawns could look so much different. So much nicer.

VINE STREET'S BORING, Olive texted.

I smiled.

SO R U GOING TO BE OK? she wrote again.

YEAH.

K. I GOTTA GO. MOM WANTS ME TO CLEAN KITCHEN. GRRR!

I WISH I MAY, I WISH I MIGHT, I texted.

HAVE THE WISH I WISH TONIGHT, Olive finished. It was the way we always said good night, the last text of the day, no matter where we were, or what was going on. Our individual wishes were never spoken aloud; they were ours alone. But it was enough that Olive understood that I had one—and that I knew she had one too.

I snapped my phone shut.

"Good night, Olive," I whispered.

* * *

That night I dreamed about the time Momma took me to the park and I fell off the swing and knocked out my front tooth. My mouth was full of warm, salty blood, and Momma was crying. I woke up with a yell, my hands and neck sweaty, and stared at the ceiling until I remembered where I was again.

Like all the dreams I had of Momma these days, I hadn't been able to make out her face. I knew it was Momma, but her features—the round brown eyes, long nose with a tiny freckle on the left-hand side, the dimple in her chin—never came into focus.

I couldn't understand it. Her face was always turned away, looking in another direction, almost as if she was afraid to look at me.

8

Technically, summer school didn't start until the end of the month. But Movado the Avocado had sent a letter to the house, informing Dad and me that due to "particular circumstances," I was to arrive at the school no later than eight thirty the following week.

She was already sitting at her desk when I walked in at 8:40, writing something on her calendar and sucking on a butterscotch square. She kept a huge container of butterscotch candies on the corner of her desk and refilled it whenever it got low. No student ever asked for—or received—a piece of her butterscotch.

She glanced at the clock as I sat down behind one of the desks. "I did say eight thirty, didn't I, May?" Again, with that regular voice she had used inside Principal Mola's office. It was so weird.

I shrugged and looked around. The classroom was empty. "Maybe. I don't remember."

"Oh, I think you do. You may not be aware of this, but punctuality is a sign of respect. I won't tolerate another late start, is that understood? If you are late tomorrow, you're going to have to face the consequences."

"Got it." I looked around at the empty classroom. "Where is everyone?"

Movado the Avocado stood up. Her pear shape was draped in a light blue cotton dress that skimmed her knees. "We're all here."

"What do you mean, 'We're all here'?" I looked around frantically. "Where are the other kids?"

"There are no other kids," Movado the Avocado said calmly. "It's just you and me." She opened a drawer inside her desk, took out a pen, and wrote something down on a sheet of paper.

"Just you and me?" I was aghast.

"That's right." My English teacher put her pen down. Behind her, I could see the edges of the crude avocado drawing I had sprayed on the wall next to her chalkboard. The words "What's fat and short and green all over?" curved over the top of it, a sloppy arch of spitefulness.

Beneath it was the answer: "Movado the Avocado!!!!!"

"This is like a joke, right?" I stood up and sidled toward the door. "I get it. Ha. Ha. Good one, Miss Movado. You totally got me."

Movado the Avocado locked eyes with mine. Her hair was arranged in its usual neat nest of curls, and she had on a pair of silver earrings that somehow matched the blue in her dress. "Your days will be divided as follows," she said calmly. "You might want to write this down so you don't forget it." She held her pen out, along with a sheet of loose-leaf paper.

I took them both. Slowly.

"Summer school, as you know, is only four hours a day, which means that you get to leave every afternoon at twelve thirty. *Unless* you come in late. For every minute you come in late in the mornings, you will have to make up that time in the afternoon. Is that understood?"

I just looked at her.

"Good. Now, for the first two hours of the day, you will be doing manual labor, which is really the whole reason why I've asked you to come early. I've decided that since you have to paint over your artwork anyway, you may as well just redo my whole room." She sighed and looked around, her eyes lingering in each corner. "Every summer I ask Pete to repaint my room, and every summer he says he will. Then I come back in September, and nothing's been done. *Nothing.*" She fixed her gaze on me again. "This is the perfect opportunity to get it completed, once and for all."

I put my pen down. "You can't use me as your personal slave!"

"The *second* two hours of your day," Movado the Avocado continued, "will be devoted to classwork. Specifically, I've decided that we will refocus on the poetry chapter you cheated your way through, and the journal you refused to write in all year."

"This is crazy!" I sputtered. "You cannot make me do all of this! It's way too much!"

"Well, you're right about one thing," Movado the Avocado said. "I can't make you do any of this, May. The choice is yours."

"This—this is like—blackmail or something!" I was so angry that my hands were actually shaking. Heat slid up the sides of my neck like a fever. I threw my pen down on the ground. Shoved the sheet of paper to the floor. It was all I could think of to do.

Movado the Avocado sat back down in her seat. She made a little roof out of the tips of her fingers and rested her chin on top of them. "Are you done?"

I glared at her. Stella Rensellaer, who lived on the other end of Ransom Street, had gotten expelled from our school right at the beginning of the year, after setting a garbage can on fire. She was pregnant now, and on welfare. Other kids went to different schools after being expelled, but they had the "mark" on them. They were always branded as troublemakers. Still, maybe expulsion would be better than this. This . . . I didn't know *what* this was. It was insane.

"May?" Movado the Avocado asked. "I asked you a question. Are you done?"

I breathed in and out through my nose like a bull.

Sat down.

"Yes," I said. *I hate you.*

"Good," Movado the Avocado said. "Then let's get to work."

9

SHE'S NUTS! I texted Olive on my way home that afternoon. WHACKED! OUT-OF-HER-MIND CRAZY! It was almost one o'clock. The sun was directly overhead, bearing down on me like a million-degree spotlight. Underneath my T-shirt, I could feel rivulets of sweat running down my back. As promised, Movado the Avocado had kept me the extra ten minutes to make up for being late this morning. And she'd started on the whole manual labor thing with a vengeance, pulling a roll of blue tape out of her bottom desk drawer and showing me how to smooth it along the bottoms of the windowsills and the blackboard and the shelves along her walls. The tape was supposed to keep the paint drips off the stuff that wasn't supposed to be painted. Movado the Avocado's room was probably the size of our entire apartment. It was going to take me a week to get it all taped up, probably another three to paint it. My back ached just thinking about it.

Afterward, for the class part of the day, she'd made me copy all the journal prompts into a new notebook. I was going to have to answer them throughout the rest of the summer—for homework.

Yeah.

Right.

WHERE R U? Olive texted back. CAN U COME TO MY HOUSE?

I HAVE TO CHECK ON GRAM. C U IN 20.

Gram was sleeping, her solitaire game spread out next to her. A cold cup of tea—still filled to the brim—was balanced on top of her lap. Next to it was a piece of toast, the edges nibbled at like a mouse. I took the teacup and the toast, dumped them into the sink, and washed the cup out. I wrote her a note, telling her I'd be at Olive's, and pulled up her sheet. My hand bumped into something hard as I tucked it around her. I pulled out the picture of Momma, the one Gram kept on her desk, and looked at it for a minute. Momma was holding Rogan when he was still a puppy, long before we'd had to give him away. Rogan was the size of a rabbit, and so small that his eyes were still closed. Momma was bent over him, her face in profile, stroking the back of his neck with her fingers. She'd loved Rogan intensely, probably because she could hold and nuzzle him all day long. She used to do that with me until I had gotten too big. By the time I was eight, just sitting on her lap hurt her back.

I put the picture back on Gram's desk, facedown, and walked out.

Olive held out a little sack of sunflower seeds as I finished telling her the details of my day with Movado the Avocado. I was sprawled out on her bed on my stomach, my elbows jammed in against her soft, blue comforter. Olive had a bedroom to die for. She really did. I wasn't one of those girls who pined over things like matching curtains and bed ruffles, but that kind of stuff looked good in Olive's room. Everything was blue, but in different shades. Her comforter was midnight blue, her rug a periwinkle blue, the walls a pale, sky blue. Olive's mother had even let her paint clouds on her walls, so that it seemed as if you were looking outside. And everything was always so *neat*. I've never really minded the fact that I'm basically a first-class slob, but it does feel nice to walk into a room where everything has its place.

"I've never heard of a teacher forcing a student to paint

her *entire* room, including the trim on the windows," Olive said. "That is kind of a lot. I wonder if she's breaking any child-labor laws."

She put the sunflower seeds down and went over to her dresser, where she started fiddling with a stack of CDs.

"She's probably breaking *all* of them," I said, cramming a handful of seeds into my mouth. "Not that she'd care or anything. She just wants to make my life miserable."

Olive held up a Beatles CD. "The *White Album*? Or *Abbey Road*?" Olive was obsessed with all things Beatles. As in, she wanted to marry Paul McCartney, even though the guy is, like, eighty years old now and totally gross. And she had a full-size poster of John Lennon taped to her ceiling so she could stare at it before she went to sleep. Personally, I didn't get it. I mean, have you ever *seen* John Lennon?

"Whatever." I groaned, rolling over on my back. "Do you ever *consider* playing anything except the Beatles, Olive?"

"The *White Album* it is," Olive said, inserting the disk into her CD player. Strains of guitar and hollow drums filled the room. She started jumping up and down. "Back in the U.S.S.R.!" she yelled, waving her arms over her head. "You don't know how lucky you are!"

I grinned. I always complained when Olive played a

Beatles CD, but once the record started, I realized I didn't really mind their music that much. They *were* old, but a lot of their songs were sort of fun. I liked a few of them. And there was actually one that they wrote about a blackbird that I might have even loved.

"We're trying to discuss my situation!" I yelled above the music. "Can you at least turn it down?"

Olive reached over and lowered the volume.

"*Thank* you." I scrambled to my knees, reached for the sunflower sack again, and scooped my hair into a ponytail. "Now, like I was saying, we have got to find a way out of this. Movado is totally abusing her power. It's not right."

"I don't know," Olive said. "I mean, it *is* a lot, but I think you should just do it, May. Seriously. I'm not trying to be a jerk here, but you did spray paint her wall." She shrugged. "You do stuff like that, you gotta deal with the consequences, you know? Besides, it'll be over before you know it."

"That's easy for you to say," I retorted. "You're not Movado the Avocado's little maid for the next three months."

"That's a little bit dramatic, don't you think?" Olive was playing a set of air drums as she talked to me.

I arched my back. "Olive. Geez, gimme a break here. Don't you feel the tiniest bit sorry for me?"

"Well, yeah!" Olive said. Her hands moved faster and faster to the beat of the drums. "Of course I do. But I'm just saying . . . you know . . . complaining about it isn't going to help. Attitude is everything, May. My mom always says that things turn out best for people who make the best of the way things turn out."

"But it's too *much*!" I wailed. "She's having me tape all her windows and the baseboards, and the shelves, *and* her blackboard, then I have to do a coat of primer, and then I have to do two coats of paint! The punishment totally does not fit the crime. Don't you think somebody should at least look into it? I mean, what if Principal Mola found out what she was doing?"

"I'm sure he knows," Olive said. Her hands slowed as the song came to an end. "Don't you think? I mean, Movado's obviously already gotten permission to get you in there early. Plus, you're her only summer school student, which means someone else had to be involved. I mean, she can't just *do* that on her own. Principal Mola's gotta know what her plans are."

I sat there for a minute, deliberating this. Sometimes it really sucked to have such a practical voice in our conversation. It blew the sympathy card right out the window.

"Yeah." I sighed heavily.

The room went quiet again as the familiar strains of

the blackbird song hovered in the air. Olive and I listened as Paul McCartney's voice floated out from the stereo, spare and soft. The song was about a blackbird with broken wings who was trying to learn how to fly again. Olive told me once that the song had been written during the civil rights movement. She said it was really about a black lady who had just gotten her freedom back and was trying to make a life for herself again.

But I never thought about the civil rights movement or the black lady when I heard it. I always thought about Momma. Especially the words, "All your life, you were only waiting for this moment to be free." Momma was free now—away from all of us, doing her own thing, wherever she was.

Sometimes I wondered if Olive knew what I was really thinking about when the song came on. She'd talked to Momma only twice that year before Momma left, once when she'd stopped by after school to pick up her history notebook I'd borrowed, and again when Gram invited her to stay for dinner one night. Momma had been lying on the couch both times, the blue and green afghan draped over her thin frame, watching Gram, who was bustling around in the kitchen. Her face was pinched tight from the pain in her back, and her hand trembled when she stuck it out to shake Olive's. She'd been pleasant enough, smiling and talking to Olive for a few moments, but afterward she'd gone into her room and shut the door. I didn't talk about Momma's back situation with anybody—not even my friends. That was Momma's business, not theirs. But Olive asked so many questions that night, especially when Momma did not come out of her room to eat dinner with Gram and me, that I finally explained the whole situation to her.

"So even though she injured her back as a teenager, she's still in constant pain?" Olive asked as I finished. "All these years later?"

"Olive." I snuck a look at Gram, hoping she wasn't getting annoyed. Gram never brought up Momma's past—or the accident. "It was a really terrible injury. She broke, like, three vertebrae in her spine. She's lucky she can even walk."

Olive chewed her meat slowly. "Holy cow."

"She has excellent medication," Gram said suddenly, spearing a piece of asparagus on the tines of her fork. "The pain only starts when the medicine wears off."

Olive shook her head and stared down at her plate. "That must be awful. I can't even imagine."

"Actually," Gram said brusquely, "it's not awful at all. It's just the way it is. Sometimes life deals you a hand that you're not quite sure how to play. But that doesn't mean you step out of the game. You just have to learn a different set of rules. Adjust to a different playing field." She chewed steadily, watching Olive as she spoke.

I held my breath, sure that Olive was going to cast her eyes down and wriggle uncomfortably under Gram's stare. But she only nodded, her eyebrows high on her forehead. "My mother says that very thing to some of her clients," she said. "More or less."

"Good," Gram said. "Then you understand."

Sometimes I wondered if Olive really understood, though.

Especially a few months after that dinner, when she heard about Momma's decision to leave.

I thought about this now as the blackbird song came to an end.

Afterward, just like always, it was like I had to remember how to breathe all over again.

10

The clock said 8:36 the next morning when I burst into Movado the Avocado's room. "I ran the whole way." I leaned over, gripping my knees with both hands, as I struggled for breath. "I did. I swear."

"Fine." Movado the Avocado stood up from her chair and handed me the roll of blue tape. "You're still four minutes late, which means you have to stay until four minutes after twelve."

"I'm *sorry*!" I said. "I just told you I ran the entire way! What else do you want me to do?"

"Get up earlier," Movado the Avocado said mildly. "That way, you won't have to run." She was dressed in her usual green attire today—an emerald green top with ruffles down the front, and khaki pants. An avocado on a stick. I snatched the tape out of her hand. "You can start on the sides of that back window," Movado the Avocado said, turning back around to her desk.

She pulled off the top to her butterscotch candy jar and took one out. The inside of my mouth salivated as she peeled off the wrapper and stuck the candy in her mouth. I hadn't had a chance to eat breakfast—I almost never did—and I usually paid the price for it right around now. "And remember to keep the tape as straight as possible. If it's crooked, you'll have to do it over again." Movado the Avocado dismissed me with a flutter of her hand. "Go on, now. You're not going to get anything done while you stand there staring at me."

I walked toward the back of the room, wondering if it was possible to hate a human being as much as I hated my English teacher at that moment. Was there any way I could get away with locking her in her closet and running out of the room? I'd have to figure out a way to get her into the closet, of course, without arousing her suspicion. That was too complicated. I kicked a chair in the last row of desks instead, and peeked over my shoulder. No response from the front of the room.

The saga with the blue tape began. Just like yesterday, it started out fine enough. Nice, straight, easy lines. Today, however, I had to do the sides of the windows. They were straight lines too, but for some reason, working vertically was throwing me off. The farther down I went, the more twisted the tape became. The tiny wrinkles that began to form at the top turned into gigantic ropy ones in the middle, until I had to peel off the strip of tape at the beginning and start all over again. By the third time, I'd had enough. Yanking the strip of tape off the wall, I threw it to the floor and hopped down off the desk.

"Problem?" Movado the Avocado asked, looking up from her book.

"Yes," I answered sarcastically. "Yes, there's a *problem.* This friggin' tape . . ." My words trailed off as she raised her finger.

"You are not going to speak to me in that tone of voice," she said. "And you are not going to use those kinds of words, either, when you address me. Change your tone, please, and your vocabulary."

I gritted my teeth. *Just get through it,* Olive had said. *Just do it.* I took a deep breath. "This tape is not going on straight. I don't know how to do it so it doesn't wrinkle."

Movado the Avocado got up from her chair. She walked over to me and took the tape out of my hands. "You have to keep the tape very close to the roll. Like this. You're stretching your pieces much too far, which is why they're wrinkling. Keep it short, and you'll be able to control it better." She handed the tape back to me and looked at the clock. "Keep going," she said. "You've still got one hour and forty-two minutes left to work on it."

I stared hatefully at the back of her as she walked over to her desk. Just for a moment, I wished I had some kind of laser-beam vision that would sear a hole through the middle of her. If I had webs that shot out of the middle of my palms, I would spin her up tightly in one, and toss her down a deep, dark hole.

She sat back down and opened her butterscotch jar. "You're not going to get anything done looking in this direction," she said, nodding at the window. "Chop-chop!"

I turned back around. *Chop-chop,* I thought. *How I'd love to chop-chop you.*

11

A muscle in my neck throbbed as I sat down at one of the desks. The labor part of the morning was over, thank goodness, and I had completed two of the four windows. I also had a stiff neck and fingers to show for it. Now I had to sit here for another two hours and listen to Movado the Avocado yammer on about the value of her precious journal and all the glorious aspects of stupid poetry.

I sighed and flipped open the notebook she had given me yesterday. It had a green cover and a wire spiral edge. Inside, as per yesterday's instructions, I had copied down all the prompts she read aloud to me, two to a page, underlined neatly. I was supposed to have answered the first two for homework.

Movado the Avocado came up behind me as I stared down at the first page.

What's your favorite time of day? What do you like the most about it?

Halfway down was the second prompt: *Describe your favorite breakfast. Who would make it for you? Where would you eat it?*

I hadn't answered either of them. They were dumb, dumb, dumb.

"I did ask you to complete the first two prompts for homework last night," she said. "Didn't I?"

I shrugged. "I forgot." This was a lie, of course. After leaving Olive's house, I'd gone home to stay with Gram. We'd watched *Wheel of Fortune* and *Jeopardy!* and *Entertainment Tonight* on the TV in her room. I'd made Gram a cup of tea (which she didn't drink), and then sat in my room fooling around with Sherman until Dad got home. He'd brought burgers and fries for dinner, and we sat at the kitchen table and ate them out of the oily white bag in silence. It was a quiet night. And I hadn't felt like ruining it by doing homework.

"You shouldn't even be giving homework," I said plaintively. "It's bad enough that I have to go to school in the summer."

Movado the Avocado sat down in one of the student

desks across from me. She folded her hands and placed them carefully in front of her. Her nails were neatly filed into small squares. No polish. On her fourth finger was a small blue ring. "Let's get something straight here, May, once and for all. *I* am the teacher. *You* are the student, which means that you do not get to make any of the rules. If I give you something for homework, I expect you to do it. And if you do not do it, you will have to face . . ."

"The *consequences*," I chimed in. "I know, I know."

Movado the Avocado leaned in. Her nostrils flared. "But you don't know. For some reason, no matter how many chances I seem to give you, it is still not sinking in."

I picked up my pencil and jammed the tip of it against the paper. "Whatever."

"This is exactly the kind of attitude you had all year." Movado the Avocado sat back in her chair and twiddled her thumbs. "Complete apathy. Blatant, defiant disregard for any and all instructions."

I yawned.

"Get up!" Movado the Avocado said.

"What?"

"Get up!" She stood up. "Out of your seat! Now!"

I stood up. Put my hand on my hip. Waited.

"Twenty jumping jacks," she said. "Right here. Right now."

I squinted. *"What?"*

"You heard me. Twenty jumping jacks. We need to get your blood flowing. Get those synapses inside your brain up and jumping so you can think clearly." She clapped her hands twice. "Come on. Let's go."

I grinned at her. Crossed my arms. "No way."

"Now."

"NO."

She gazed at me for one long minute. I let her, making no move to wipe what I hoped was a very hostile grin off my face. It was kind of funny, the way teachers thought they could just rip you around. They were older, they'd been to college and gotten some dumb degree, so they thought they could just tell the rest of us to jump and we would cringe and ask how high. Well, not this time. Not this girl.

"Get out." The command was so quiet that for a moment I wasn't sure if I'd heard her correctly.

"What?"

"You heard me," Movado the Avocado said. "Get out. I have more important things to do than waste my time—my *summer*—trying to help you."

Something cold ran through the bottom of my belly.

"I mean it." She stood up. "Leave." She walked over to her desk. "I thought maybe if we worked one-on-one together, if I gave you my undivided attention . . ." She let the words trail off, shaking her head. "It doesn't matter. I can't work with someone who doesn't want to change. And I'm sorry that I thought I could. So leave."

I put my hand back on my hip. "If I leave, are you going to have Principal Mola expel me?"

Movado the Avocado's black eyes narrowed. "Someday, May, you are going to have to think about someone other than yourself."

"Okay," I said. "But if I walk out this door, am I going to be able to come back to this school next year?"

She licked her lips slowly, as if there were still traces of the butterscotch candy on them. "Yes. You will be able to come back next year."

I stood there. Bit my bottom lip. Peeled at the skin around my thumb.

"LEAVE!" she said. "I mean it, May! Now!"

"Fine." I lifted my arm, tried to make my voice light as I turned on one heel. "Adios."

"Adios," I heard Movado the Avocado say as I made my way out her classroom door. "*Hasta la vista*, baby."

12

"What'd you do, hit her?" Olive was leaning against her bookshelf, eating pistachio nuts out of a small plastic sleeve. She was still in her pajamas. "You hit her, didn't you?"

"No, I didn't *hit* her." I sank down into her desk chair. "God, Olive, I'm not crazy, you know."

I'd gone over to Olive's as soon as Movado the Avocado let me go. It was only ten thirty in the morning, but the Beatles were already crooning "Sgt. Pepper's Lonely Hearts Club Band" softly in the background. Olive's parents were at work; we had the place to ourselves. "So what did happen?" Olive asked.

"Honestly, I don't even know. She just told me to go. So I went."

"Out of the blue," Olive said, fingering another pistachio out of the bag. "With no argument or anything?"

I shrugged. "I guess we had an argument. Kind of. It was so stupid. She told me to stand up and do jumping jacks so that my blood could start moving."

"Why?" Olive asked. "Did you look tired? Were you yawning or something?"

I glared at her. "I might've yawned. A little." Olive popped another pistachio into her mouth. "Anyway, when I told her I wouldn't do the jumping jacks, she flipped. Told me to get out."

"So does that mean you're back to square one?" Olive sat down on the end of her bed and handed me the pistachios. "Are they going to expel you now?"

"No." I leaned over the chair. "I asked her that exact question. I said, 'If I leave, are you going to have me expelled?' And she said no."

"Just like that. She said no. No more summer school. No expulsion. Everything's just dropped."

"YES!" I flung my arms up into the air gleefully. "Just like that!" Olive's steady expression did not change. I dropped my arms, embarrassed. "Anyway, it's over. I don't even care."

Olive raised her eyebrows and then turned around, flipping through her CDs.

"*What?*" I asked. "Why're you always like looking at me like that?"

"Like what?" Olive asked.

"Like . . . I don't know. Like you're judging every move I make."

"I'm not judging you," Olive said. She slid one of the CDs out from the bottom of the pile and studied the back. It was *Magical Mystery Tour*—one of her favorite Beatle albums. "You're the one who wanted to come over here and tell me the good news."

"See, like right there." I stood up, knocking over Olive's chair. "You're being totally sarcastic when you say 'good news.' Why do you do that?"

Olive shrugged. She was still reading the list of songs on the back of the CD. "Well, do *you* think it's good news?"

"Of course it's good news!" I was yelling now, but I didn't care. "What else would it be? You're acting like I just told you that I ran her over with a *car* or something!"

"May." Olive looked up finally. "Chill, okay? I'm on your side here."

I could feel the veins along the sides of my neck pulsing, a knot in the back of my throat getting bigger and bigger. This always happened when I got angry. During the argument with Brittany Martinson, I'd gotten so worked up so fast that I actually started sweating. Afterward, it had been hard to swallow, almost as if a fist had lodged itself somewhere between my throat and chest. Now I took a deep breath. "I know." I ran my fingertips lightly over the top of my head. "Sorry. I guess sometimes it doesn't really feel like you are."

"Well, I am," Olive said. "So relax."

I hung around for a little while after that, but it was like all the air had gone out of me. Olive's lack of excitement about my news had flattened it a little. And now, instead of sitting on top of the world the way I had felt running over to her place, I felt as if I had been transferred over to a hill of some kind, where the grass was too slippery to stand, the clouds overhead a little too high out of reach.

"I gotta go," I said finally, getting up from Olive's bed.

"Go where?" she asked.

Nowhere. But I didn't want to be here, either.

"Gram needs me," I lied. "She isn't feeling so good."

"Oh." Olive looked at me out of the corner of her eye. "I'll call you later, then."

13

I think I have some kind of switch inside me. If it gets turned on, all my anger and boiling mad thoughts start heating up like a tea kettle. When it gets turned off, they settle back down. Lately, my switch has been turned on more often than not, and by the time I left Olive's house and reached Ransom Street, the little tea kettle inside my chest was at a full boil, screaming at the top of its lungs.

"I'm home!" I yelled, storming past Gram's room. "Let me know when you want your tea!"

It wasn't even noon yet, but the heat in my room was already like the inside of an oven. My fan, which was balanced unsteadily on top of an upside-down milk crate, had been turned off. Stupid Dad. He was obsessed with not wasting electricity. Every morning, before he left for work, he walked through the apartment and turned off all the fans and all the lights. Except in Gram's room, of course. He never went into Gram's room.

I walked over and turned the fan on high, which was the highest speed I was allowed to use. The plastic frame rattled. I turned the knob to extra high. The fan wobbled as the dusty blades spun frantically inside of it—and then fell over with a resounding *clunk*. Two seconds later, Mr. Reynolds's broom handle sounded on the ceiling: *Rap, rap, rap.*

Something exploded inside my chest. I grabbed the fan and threw it across the room. It crashed against the side of my desk and then plunked heavily to the floor. My ratty beanbag chair became airborne, skittering across the top of my bed, landing in a heap next to it. My arms and feet moved with a mind of their own, slicing through the air like violent propellers, making contact with whatever was in their way. Books, papers, my harmonica, dirty clothes, empty plastic cups, even an old banana peel flew in all different directions. In the span of a few seconds, my room had become a blizzard of flying objects. Inside his cage, poor Sherman scuttled to and fro, frightened by all the noise.

And then it was over.

I stood in the middle of the wreckage, breathing heavily, and surveyed the damage. It was pretty bad. My room was usually a mess, but right now it looked like a tornado had hit it. And the worst part was, the heaviness inside my chest hadn't eased. Not even a little bit.

I turned as a faint tapping sounded on my door. "May?"

Gram. She sounded frightened.

I wanted to cry. Instead I opened the door slowly.

Her face was pale. "Are you all right, honey?"

I swallowed over the lump in my throat. "Yeah, Gram." I stepped out of my room, shutting the door behind me carefully. "I'm okay. My bookshelf fell down. That's all. Come on. I'll make you some tea."

She leaned heavily on my arm as I led her out to the kitchen. Her pink slippers shuffled against the floor. "It got so loud," she said. "I was worried."

We both stopped as a sharp rapping sounded on the front door. "Hello?" It was Mr. Reynolds. "What in God's name is going on in there?" He rapped again, harder this time. "Hello? Someone better open this door and explain things, or I'm going to call the—"

I yanked open the door. Mr. Reynolds was a very short man. I had never seen him dressed in anything other than the dark pair of pants he had on now, a dirty white T-shirt, and bright red suspenders. His dark mustache was so thin that sometimes I wondered if he had actually drawn it over his upper lip with a permanent marker. "Mr. Reynolds," I said, "I'm sorry. My bookcase fell over and everything just sort of crashed down around it. It's all straightened up now, though. I'm sorry."

Mr. Reynolds peered around me, as if he expected to see a roomful of pit bulls straining on their leashes. "Well, all right," he said finally. "By God, I thought some kind of an army had charged in here."

"No army," Gram said from the kitchen. "We're fine. You can go back downstairs now, Walt."

"All right." Mr. Reynolds turned around grudgingly and started down the stairs. "I don't know what it's gonna take to get it through your heads up here that the walls in this place are like paper. I can hear everything. *Everything*." He muttered under his breath all the way down.

I closed the door and leaned against it for a moment.

"You sure you're okay?" Gram asked.

"Yeah," I said. "Just tired."

"You go on," Gram said. "Lie down. You look like you could use a rest. Besides, I don't want tea. I'm just going to have a glass of water."

"You should have tea," I said. "Dad said the caffeine is good for you."

Gram held up her hand. "I don't want tea. If I drink

another cup of tea, I'm going to turn into a tea bag. Now you go on, May. Go lie down. Take a nap. Then we'll talk about dinner."

"You sure?"

"I'm sure." Gram's voice was firm.

I walked toward my room. "Gram?" I asked. "Can I ask you a question?"

"Of course," she said.

"How do you know . . ." I paused, picking at the paint on the doorknob. "How do you know if you should stick with something? Even if you think it's unfair?"

Gram looked puzzled for a moment. Then she drew her fingers across the wrinkly surface of her forehead. "I think that depends on the situation," she said finally. "How unfair is unfair?"

I looked down at the floor. Stepped hard on the toe of my shoe. "Sorta unfair," I said.

"Well," Gram said, closing the top of her housecoat, "I would think that's for you to answer, then."

"Yeah." I wrinkled my nose. "Okay. Thanks."

Adults always gave answers like that.

It was their way of saying they had no idea either.

14

I lay down flat on my bed, right in the middle of the mess. It was hard to get comfortable among the lumps of thrown clothing and shoes and books strewn around, but I didn't move. Not for a long, long time.

Once, at the beach, Momma had done a cartwheel. Right out of nowhere. Just to do it. Along the horizon, the sky had started to change from a light blue to a deep purple color. The waves were soft, lapping the shore like tiny kitten tongues, and white sandpipers skittered to and fro, leaving prints along the damp sand. We'd been heading back to the beach house, which we rented for a week every summer back then. I was in Dad's arms, wrapped in a red-and-white-striped towel. My Little Mermaid bathing suit was still wet.

"May!" Momma had shouted behind us. "Watch me!"

Dad turned just as she lifted her arms and tilted forward.

"Elizabeth!" he said. "Don't!"

But her legs came up over her, and like a windmill, she turned upside down into a cartwheel, landing upright in the sand. The smile on her face was huge—but fleeting. She collapsed in a heap.

Dad rushed down to her, still holding me. "Elizabeth!" he shouted. She moaned, writhing in the sand, her eyes glassy with pain. "Why would you do something like that?" Dad cried. "I *told* you!"

He'd had to put me down to lift her. I held on to the hem of his blue bathing suit as he half ran, half walked through the dunes. Momma's arm hung down limply behind him, like a doll's. The lifelessness of it frightened me. We had to take her to a hospital. She'd reinjured her back. It wasn't nearly as serious as the original injury, after which she'd had to stay in the hospital wrapped in a body cast for six weeks—but it had damaged an already strained ligament. We'd had to leave the beach two days early.

Now I squeezed my eyes shut, trying to remember another time when Momma's face had lit up again the way it had for those few seconds after the cartwheel. But nothing came. Most days her face had been clamped tight with pain, since the slightest thing—an abrupt turn, getting up from the couch the wrong way, even standing in the supermarket line for too long—could send her back into spasms. The only thing that eased the tightness around her mouth or the muscles in her jaw was her medicine, which made her eyes look vacant and hollow.

I closed my eyes. I didn't want either picture inside my head.

I hated remembering her that way.

It made me furious.

Outside my window, the light began to change, shifting from a dull yellow to a muted gray. I could hear the sound of cars pulling into driveways, and the pounding of a basketball against the street. A man's voice yelled for someone named Shirley. Across the street, a little boy shrieked, "Daddy's home!"

After a while, I fell asleep.

When I woke up, the back of my neck was ribboned with sweat. Two soupy puddles had pooled inside my bra. I sat up slowly and ran my fingers along an indent in my cheek from lying on a wrinkled sheet. Momma's face used to look like that when she slept too long. Trails of shallow, pink wrinkles under her hooded eyes.

I reached for my harmonica. Breathed in and out as

the soft, mournful sound of "Moon River" filled my ears. Sometimes I tried to imagine the notes of "Moon River"—the music itself—knitting itself into a kind of blanket as I played. Note after note created another stitch, an additional row of soft wool so that as I finished, as the last note sounded and then drifted out the window, I was able to curl up inside, put my head down, and stay very, very still.

It was warm in there, inside that blanket of notes, for a little while.

Sometimes it almost felt okay again.

Almost.

15

I walked back into Movado the Avocado's room the next morning at 8:32. She was reading a book at her desk, her chin mashed into her fist. I knocked on the door lightly. She looked up. An expression crossed her face: surprise? shock? satisfaction? I couldn't tell. "Yes?" she asked.

"I'd . . ." I hadn't prepared a speech. Honestly, I'd kind of expected her to jump up and say something like, *May! You're back!* "I . . . um . . . was thinking maybe I could try this again," I said. "I mean, if you're up for it."

Movado the Avocado sat back in her chair. *"Really."* It was a statement, not a question.

I bristled. "Yeah. Really."

"And what, may I ask, brought about this sudden change of heart?"

I ran my tongue over my teeth. If she thought I'd dragged myself all the way back here just so that she could sit and watch me squirm, she could forget it. But she was still staring at me, waiting for an answer.

I shrugged. "I don't know. Nothing, really. I just think . . . I should."

Movado the Avocado nodded. There was an odd expression on her face, a little smile or smirk. I couldn't make it out. But it was exactly the kind of look she had given me that day in class when she humiliated me. In front of everyone. "You know what?" I said. "Just forget it. I can't."

She lowered her chin. "Now you *can't*? Why not?"

"Because I hate your guts!" I burst out. "I'd rather get kicked out of a million schools than have to stay in this room with you all summer! You're miserable and nasty and you humiliate all your students, because you want to make everyone around you feel as crappy as you do!"

Now Movado the Avocado stood up from her seat. Slowly, as if a string in the ceiling was pulling her up. "*Humiliate* all my students?" she repeated.

"Yes! Like you did with me! Laughing at my answer and making me feel like a total idiot because I didn't know what that dumb poem meant!"

Movado the Avocado closed her book with one finger and placed her palm on top of it. "What poem?"

I gestured futilely with my hands. "I don't know . . . that retarded one about some raisin in the sun. . . . I don't remember."

"You mean 'Harlem'?" she asked. "By Langston Hughes?"

"I don't *remember*," I said sullenly. "I'm stupid, in case you forgot."

Movado the Avocado touched her shirt lightly with two fingers. "I never said you were stupid, May."

"You didn't have to." I shoved my hands into my pockets. "You laughed at my answer. Everyone knew what you thought."

Movado the Avocado drew her eyebrows in until they formed a slightly spiky, continuous line. "I didn't laugh at you," she said. "I would never laugh at a student."

I glared at her. *"You. Laughed."*

The only sound in the room was the dull buzzing of the fluorescent lights overhead. I looked out the window. The football players were doing drills in the middle of the stadium, running up and down the length of the field. They had practice all summer, sometimes in the evening, too.

Movado the Avocado cleared her throat. "Is that why you drew that thing on my wall?" she asked quietly.

I looked away from the football players, stared at the

floor. Used the tip of my shoe to kick at the black nub of the rubber doorstop.

"May?"

"I don't know. Maybe."

Movado the Avocado reached up and touched one of the green ruffles on her shirt with two fingers. "Well . . . ," she said. "I thought you were just being mean."

I looked up at her. "It *was* mean."

"Yes," Movado the Avocado concurred. "It was."

We locked eyes.

"You still want to come back?" she asked.

I nodded. Slowly.

"And you're going to try this time?"

I nodded again.

"Okay." She held out the blue tape. I walked toward it slowly and took it.

Undid the blue tape just a tiny bit, the way she had showed me.

"Short pieces," Movado the Avocado said.

I smiled the merest bit. "I know."

16

The windows were finished. There were still some wrinkles in the blue tape, but Movado the Avocado had given it the okay. Tomorrow I would start taping the base-boards. After that, it would be time to start the primer. I wasn't actually looking forward to painting, but I was anxious to be done with the blue tape. I was starting to see stripes of blue wherever I looked. Now I sat down at one of the desks and opened my green notebook.

"You did the first prompt," Movado the Avocado said, leaning over the top of the desk opposite me. She looked pleased. "Good for you."

I'd answered the first prompt last night, after eating din-ner with Dad. He'd brought home bean burritos from Taco Bell and four bottles of orange Gatorade. We'd eaten in silence. Again. *My favorite time of day is lunch. I am usually starving by the time lunch comes around, so it's a good time.*

"I just don't understand these prompts. I never know if I'm writing the right thing. And they're so . . . dumb." I glanced at Movado the Avocado quickly. "No offense or anything."

"They're not meant to be rocket science," Movado the Avocado said. "And there is never any right answer, May. They're your words. Your thoughts. The point is just to get you writing."

"But why? Why are English teachers always so gung ho about getting us to write?"

"Because it's important," Movado the Avocado said. "You need to know how to compose a good sentence, whether in a letter, a story, or a poem. And sometimes, when you write well, you get a chance to see things in a whole different way."

"'My favorite time of day is lunch. I am usually starving by the time lunch comes around, so it's a good time.'" I repeated my words in a dull tone of voice. "That's seeing things in a whole different way?"

"Maybe not yet," Movado the Avocado said. "But it's writing. And like anything else, the more you do it, the better you'll get at it."

"I hate writing."

"Why?"

"It's boring. And hard." I tapped the side of my head. "I can never get what's in my head down on paper."

Movado the Avocado opened a bright yellow notebook that was sitting in front of her. "I have a hard time with that too."

"You do?" I sat back in my seat. "But you're an English teacher!"

"My strong suit is grammar, which you may or may not be aware of." I snorted. Movado the Avocado's other nickname was the Grammar Nazi. "But I've always struggled with writing," she continued. "I can *write*, of course. I wouldn't be teaching English if I didn't know how to *write*. But not the way I probably should. And not the way I wish I could."

"You wish you could write better?" I asked.

"Oh, yes," Movado the Avocado said. "It was always a dream of mine to become a writer."

"So why didn't you?"

She smiled. "Well, I tried. But I wasn't good enough. They said no."

"So try again."

Movado the Avocado sighed. "Oh, I've tried. I have an

entire *drawer* full of rejection slips at home. Believe me." She shook her head. "My chance at becoming an author has passed. I've accepted that. I'm an English teacher, which I enjoy, and am good at, and . . . well, that's just who I am."

I stuck my bottom lip out. It felt weird hearing about this personal side of Movado the Avocado—even if it was just a little bit.

"Anyway." Movado the Avocado fluttered a hand in front of her face, as if to dismiss everything she had just said. "This time is not going to be spent talking about me. How about the second prompt?"

"'Describe your favorite breakfast. Who would make it for you? What would you eat?'" I looked up as I finished reading it. "Cereal. I would make it."

"What kind of cereal?"

"Cocoa Krispies."

"What's the bowl look like?"

"The bowl?"

"Yes," Movado the Avocado said. "The bowl you pour the Cocoa Krispies into. What's it look like?"

I shrugged. "*I* don't know. We just have regular plastic bowls."

She stared at me for a beat. "Did you eat breakfast this morning?"

"No."

"Me either," she said. "I'm starving. You want to go get something?"

I looked at her like she was crazy. "To eat?"

"Yes." She stood up.

"Where?"

"Anywhere. Sweet Treet is right around the corner. They've got good breakfast sandwiches. Great coffee. Come on." She reached for her purse behind her desk and swung it over her shoulder.

"If I don't go with you, are you going to, like, penalize me or something?"

"You're *not* hungry?" Movado the Avocado asked.

I yanked on the neck of my T-shirt. I was starving. "Well, yeah. Kind of. But I mean . . . is this like some kind of . . . I don't know . . . *trick* or something?"

Movado the Avocado laughed. Really laughed. Like a regular person and not some insane mental patient the way she did when students asked her if she would please, just this once, consider curving the midterm. She had nice teeth. "No trick," she said. "Just a meal."

"Okay." I shrugged. "Sure."

17

Sweet Treet was a block behind the school. I'd walked by it a million times, but I'd never been inside. Honestly, it looked like an old people's kind of place, with the cement ramp that led up to the front, an orange and white plastic flower wreath hanging on the door, and a breakfast special sign that read: TWO EGGS, TOAST, BACON, AND COFFEE: ONLY $1.99. The sign, which was propped up in the front window, had been written on a cardboard sheet in small, shaky handwriting. Old people's handwriting.

So I was surprised when I followed Movado the Avocado inside. It was full of non-old people. Teenagers, even. And there was Pittsburgh Steelers paraphernalia everywhere: posters and pictures and newspaper articles and flags and articles of clothing, pinned and hung and dangling over every available free space. There was even a real Pittsburgh Steelers helmet with someone's name scribbled on the side propped up on a little wooden shelf over the cash register. I didn't know much about the Pittsburgh Steelers, but I was pretty sure old people didn't either. Maybe Sweet Treet wasn't such a bad place after all.

Movado the Avocado took a seat immediately at a small table next to the front window and looked at me. I was all for sharing a meal, but I wasn't going to be caught dead being seen eating it with Movado the Avocado. I hesitated. "Could we . . . ?"

She opened her napkin and spread it on her lap. "What's wrong?"

"Um . . ." I cleared my throat. This had to be said nicely. "Could we maybe . . . sit somewhere else? Away from the window?"

"What's wrong with the window?"

I bit my tongue. "Nothing's wrong with it, actually. It's just . . ." I glanced at the window blinds, thinking fast. "I'm allergic to dust." I lowered my voice. "And there's a lot of dust on those blinds."

Movado the Avocado frowned, peering at the blinds. I held my breath. They were actually pretty clean. "All right," she said. "Let's move to the back of the room, then. No one's going to want you sneezing all over their meal. Especially me."

I heaved a sigh of relief as we maneuvered our way through the small maze of tables toward the back of the room. The restaurant really was cute. There was a long coffee bar that ran the length of one side, complete with red swivel stools and glass sugar canisters. Every table had a tiny vase in the middle of it, filled with a single fresh daisy. And the muffins, which sat under a glass dome next to the cash register, were as big as softballs.

"So," Movado the Avocado said, once we had gotten settled. "I'm willing to bet that after you eat breakfast here, you may just change your journal entry from this morning."

I cocked my head. "Is *that* why we're here? This is a writing exercise?"

She studied her menu, which she'd slipped out from between the napkin holder and salt and pepper shakers. "Maybe."

I rolled my eyes and opened my own menu. Hidden agendas were another thing about teachers I didn't like. Mr. Crumb, our social studies teacher, was full of hidden agendas. He'd ask us random questions about the Civil War one day—in the middle of a whole other lesson—and then the next, give us a pop quiz on it. If we complained, he'd say, "What're you talking about? We just reviewed it yesterday!" I hated that.

"Have you ever been here before?" Movado the Avocado asked.

"Nope. Never."

She raised her eyebrows. "Wow. I thought everyone in Sudbury had been to Sweet Treet at least once."

My stomach growled as I looked at the menu. There were all kinds of things: pancakes with eggs, cereal, omelets, oatmeal and fruit, eggs and bacon or sausage or ham. And something called cottage fries. "What're cottage fries?" I asked.

Movado the Avocado raised her eyebrows. "Ah," she said. "*Now* you have stumbled upon the secret that is Sweet Treet. You have to order a plate of cottage fries, May. They're unlike anything you've ever tried before in your life."

"But what are they?" I pressed. "French fries?"

"Kind of. But not really. Just get them. You won't regret it."

I ordered a plate of cottage fries and a bowl of Cocoa Krispies.

Movado the Avocado ordered a mozzarella and tomato omelet, rye toast (burned, for some reason), cottage fries, and coffee.

"You're not old enough to remember," she said after the waitress had gone off with our order. "But Sweet Treet wasn't always a breakfast place. It used to be an ice cream parlor."

Fascinating. I started to pick at my thumbnail.

"I used to come here all the time with my best friend."

If Movado the Avocado knew I was bored, she either didn't show it—or she didn't care. "Every Friday after school. We'd sit right over there." She paused, nodding toward the coffee bar. "And order ourselves the most gigantic sundae in the place—the Supercalifragilisticexpialidocious Sundae. Oh my goodness, it was a sight! That sundae was bigger than the two of us standing on top of each other." She grinned. "Well, not really, but you know what I mean. It had six scoops of ice cream—all vanilla, of course. You can't have the sort of toppings the Supercalifragilisticexpialidocious Sundae had on it and not have vanilla ice cream."

I looked up. "What kind of toppings?"

Movado the Avocado closed her eyes. "Every topping you can imagine. Wet walnuts. Cherries. Pineapple. Hot fudge. Peanut butter. Bananas. Chocolate chips. Salted peanuts. Reese's Pieces."

I drew back, horrified. "That's disgusting!"

"Oh no, it was *heaven*." Movado the Avocado opened her eyes. "And the reason it was heaven was because we just ate the things we liked out of it. She ate the nuts and the bananas and the hot fudge. I ate the cherries and the pineapple and the Reese's Pieces."

"That doesn't make any sense," I said. "Why didn't you just get your own individual sundaes with the stuff you wanted on top?"

Movado the Avocado shrugged. "I guess we never really thought to," she said. "Eating it together was the best part."

The waitress came over with our plates. Movado the Avocado's was huge, filled with the omelet and toast and strange round crispy things. My plate was smaller, filled with the same round crispy things. Alongside my plate, the waitress placed a bowl, an aluminum pitcher of milk, and a mini box of Cocoa Krispies. I dumped the Cocoa Krispies into my bowl, poured milk over the top of it, and waited. I never ate a single bite of my Cocoa Krispies until the milk had turned a deep chocolate color.

"Are you going to try a cottage fry?" Movado the Avocado asked. She already had one speared on her fork. "Don't let them get cold."

I picked one up and put it in my mouth. Crunched down. Grinned as the salt and oil and crispy potato filled my mouth.

Across from me, Movado the Avocado grinned too. "Eh?" she said. "What'd I tell you? It pays to listen to your teachers, doesn't it?"

I rolled my eyes.

She laughed.

We ate for a few moments in silence, and then Movado the Avocado asked, "Who do you hang out with, May?"

"You mean friends?"

She nodded. "Didn't you used to be friends with Brittany Martinson and that whole group?"

I shrugged, hoping she didn't notice the heat under my cheeks. "Yeah. Not anymore, though." Brittany had been in English class with me this year, along with Nikki and Ashley. The four of us always sat in the corner, passing notes to one another.

"Why not?" she asked. "Did you have a falling out?"

"Sort of."

"Well, is there anyone else you like to spend time with?"

"Olive Masters," I said. "That's really about it."

"Oh, I like Olive," Movado the Avocado said. "I had her this past year for Advanced English. She was a marvelous student."

I nodded. "Yeah. She's really smart."

"She's on the honors track now, isn't she?" Movado the Avocado took a bite of her burned toast.

I didn't want to talk about Olive and her great grades right now. It made me feel stupid. "Yeah, I think so." I shifted in my seat. "Why do you eat your toast burned like that?"

"I love burned toast," Movado the Avocado answered mysteriously. "I always have, ever since I was a little girl."

"Ugh." I frowned, thinking of the charred taste of my last grilled cheese sandwich. "I think it tastes awful."

Movado the Avocado shrugged. "Well, everyone has their

own preferences. That's what makes things interesting." She held up my Cocoa Krispies box. "You think these taste pretty good, don't you?"

I nodded.

She set the box back down and shook her head slightly. "See? And I wouldn't eat those things, even if I were starving to death."

I sat up straighter in my seat. "That's just 'cause you're an adult. No adults like kids' cereal."

"Actually," she said, "it has nothing to do with it being a kids' cereal. I just think they look like hamster pellets."

Now I was really offended. "So you haven't even tried them?"

Movado the Avocado shook her head. "Nope."

I pushed the bowl across the table. "Never judge a book by its cover," I said, using one of her favorite class sayings. She looked at it for a moment and then held up a piece of her burned toast. I took it from her. Crunched down hard on it as she dipped her spoon into my cereal bowl. I kept chewing, even though it tasted like dirty cardboard. I watched Movado the Avocado's face as she swallowed a mouthful of Cocoa Krispies. "Well?" I asked finally.

"Even worse than I thought," she said.

I laughed, putting the toast down on the table. "Actually, I was thinking the exact same thing."

18

"I can't believe she took you out to eat." Olive was lying on her stomach on one of those black rubber swings, drifting back and forth. "I've never been out anywhere with a teacher before. What was it like? Didn't you feel weird?"

We were at the Charles Street Park. Sometimes when there was nothing else to do, we came here just to hang out. If a lot of little kids were all over the place, we left, but today it was completely empty. Overhead, the sun beat down like an electric tennis ball. Dust lifted up in little clouds around Olive's feet, and then settled again.

"It was pretty weird." I leaned back against the grass and looked up at the sky. "I asked her if we could sit in the back, actually. Away from that huge front window. I didn't want anybody to see us."

"Ha!" Olive giggled, and kicked herself forward. "I probably would've too." Olive and I hadn't actually talked about my decision to go back to summer school, but when she texted me earlier and I had written back, telling her where I was, she had responded with: YOU ROCK. Which had made me smile, inside and out.

"Did you know she wanted to be a writer?" I asked.

Olive turned her head. Long strands of her brown hair obscured everything but the tip of her nose. "She did?"

"Yeah. She told me that. She said she had a whole drawer full of rejection slips from the people who tell you your stuff isn't good."

"Wow." Olive braked herself with the toe of her shoe. "That's kind of sad."

"She should just keep trying, though," I said. "Don't you think?"

"I don't know." Olive got up out of the swing. "She's pretty old."

"I know." I stared at a cloud shaped like a palm tree. "It must really suck to get old. Especially if you haven't had any of your dreams come true."

"Well, that might not be the only dream she had."

I shrugged. "Maybe not."

* * *

Later I sat down on my bed and stared out the window. It had started to rain. Finally. Now maybe things would cool off a little. I reached over and pushed up the heavy sill. A gritty smell rose up from the pavement as the drops fell. I reached for my journal. Opened it to the first page. Grabbed a pencil off the floor.

My favorite breakfast is the one Gram used to make all of us on Sunday mornings. Gram's parents used to live in Ireland, so she grew up eating lots of Irish food. Every Sunday she used to make us the same breakfast her parents used to make her when she was a little girl.

Tea came first. Always. Lots of black tea, with lots of sugar. Gram says the Irish people don't drink coffee—just really strong sweet tea. Next came a plate filled with grilled tomatoes and fried eggs. After that, a basket with slices of brown bread—which Gram made from scratch—and finally, a big plate of bangers and mash. Bangers and mash are what the Irish call sausage and potatoes. And Gram's bangers and mash are the best things in the world. The sausage is crispy, and the potatoes are soft and salty. Gram *always made an onion gravy, too, which she would pour all over the potatoes, and when I took my first bite, I couldn't stop smiling. And I don't even like onions!*

I put my pencil down. It was weird how going to breakfast with Movado the Avocado had made me want to try a little. Almost as if I owed her in some small way. And I hadn't thought about bangers and mash in a long time. Actually, I couldn't even remember the last time Gram had made anything for breakfast at all. Dad left every morning before I was awake, which meant that even if I had enough time to scarf down a bowl of Cocoa Krispies, I ate them alone at the kitchen table.

Which, come to think of it, made them taste even worse than they usually did.

Even if I did let the milk get super chocolaty first.

19

Taping the baseboards turned out to be a cinch after all the complications with the windows. Working horizontally was much easier than working vertically. I finished the whole room in two hours while Movado the Avocado sat at her desk, reading a book and making her way through three pieces of butterscotch. And I was ready when it came time for the journal. I flipped it open quickly and pointed to the two paragraphs about Gram's Irish breakfast I had written the night before.

"Actually," Movado the Avocado said, "we're going to work on poetry today."

I stared at her. "But I did it! The journal, I mean! I did it! Again! For homework!"

She glanced at it. Quickly. "That's terrific, May. And

I'll be sure to read it later. But right now we're going to talk about poetry."

I slammed my notebook shut. Teachers were the most annoying, ridiculous, unpredictable, obnoxious people on the face of the earth. Period.

She looked at me out of the corner of her eye. "There is no need to slam things. You know better, May."

I slumped in my seat.

Movado the Avocado placed another notebook in front of me. This one had a bright purple cover and a spiral edge. "This will be your poetry notebook. From now on, you will need to bring your journal and your poetry notebook with you to class every day. Is that understood?"

"Yes."

"Fine." She walked back over to her desk and grabbed her purse. "Then come with me."

"I'm not hungry," I said sullenly.

"We're not eating," Movado the Avocado said. "Get up and come with me. And bring your purple notebook."

I made a huge deal about extricating myself from my chair and having to stand up, but I followed Movado the Avocado down the slick, empty hall, past the row of blue lockers, and down the wide marble steps. By now a few of the other classrooms were packed with students attending real summer school; I didn't know if I envied or pitied them. "Where are we going?" I asked again.

Movado the Avocado just made that annoying flutter movement with her fingers, this time over her shoulder. "You'll see in a minute," she answered in a singsong sort of voice. "Try to keep up, May."

20

For a short, chubby woman, Movado the Avocado could burn some serious rubber. She had on sneakers, but I was practically panting as I tried to keep pace with her. My thin rubber flip-flops were beginning to get a hole in the heel too. It wasn't comfortable.

We walked three full blocks behind the school and then turned abruptly at the end of Maple Avenue. If we went left, we'd be headed toward downtown Sudbury. Right would lead us into an enormous housing development. Movado the Avocado strode directly ahead. "Where the heck are you *going*?" I asked. "The only thing up here is the river!"

She turned around and looked at me. "Exactly. Now be careful where you step. Stay on the path here. I don't want you to get poison ivy."

I wasn't even aware we were *on* a path. I looked down. A narrow, rutted trail wound its way through a thicket of shrubs and then disappeared. I stepped carefully along it, hopping from one side to the other whenever I spotted a suspicious-looking leaf. In less than five minutes, the trail came to an end. And there, before us, sat the Susquehanna River, moving sluggishly along under the bright sunlight. The water was the color of Silly Putty, the riverbank a mess of scrubby pine and weeds.

I wrinkled my nose. "Ugh."

Movado the Avocado looked at me in surprise. "Why 'ugh'?" she asked. "Don't you think it's beautiful?"

"Beautiful?" I retorted. "Do you have any idea how disgusting this river is? How polluted it is with chemicals and stuff?"

Word was that a meat-processing plant up in Syracuse, New York, emptied all its waste into the river. Sometimes, when it got unbearable hot out, a smell like raw eggs came up from the water. Nobody I knew—especially people my age—ever set foot near the river. It was a hangout only for drunks and homeless people. Probably rats and snakes, too. I shivered.

Movado the Avocado visored her eyes with one hand. "Well we're not here to *drink* it, May."

The riverbank was littered with rocks. Behind us were

a few ugly maple trees. Their branches sagged under the heat, and their leaves were brown and crinkled. "What're we here for, then?" I asked. "To pick rocks?"

Movado the Avocado laughed. She walked over to a medium-size flat stone beneath one of the maple trees and sat down under a branch that almost touched her hair. "No, no rock picking," she said. "I just think people do a lot of good thinking next to a body of water."

"Well, then let's drive down to the ocean." I kicked a pebble under my foot. "Because this body of water is a dump."

"Sit down, May."

Grudgingly, I walked over and sat down on a rock a little ways from her. It was slightly smaller than hers, and not nearly as flat.

"Close your eyes," Movado the Avocado said.

"Why?"

"May." Her voice was final.

I closed my eyes.

"Good. Now listen."

"To what?"

"Shhh . . . Just listen."

I arranged myself on my rock, which was not an easy thing to do, since part of it was sticking into my rear end, and tried to listen.

"I don't hear anything," I said, opening my eyes.

"You have to give it a few minutes," Movado the Avocado said. "Try not to say anything for two minutes. Just listen."

I wondered if my English teacher took yoga or something at night. I peeked over at her, expecting to see her legs crossed pretzel-style in front of her and her thumbs and index fingers touching. But she was just sitting normally on the rock. Her eyes were closed, and she appeared to be concentrating. I leaned in a little, but there was no *om* sound coming out of her mouth, no incense burning anywhere. I closed my eyes again. Tried, once more, to listen.

My nose itched. I scratched it. The sound of the river was coming from somewhere in the distance. Slap. Slap. Slap. My legs were hot. So was the top of my head. A droning noise, like a steady buzz, sounded all around me. Something whistled. Two short trills, followed by a long, high one. Then again. And once more. A splash. A flutter of wings.

"Okay," Movado the Avocado said. "You can open your eyes now."

I opened my eyes. "I think I heard some stuff."

"Good!" She smiled. "What did you hear?"

"Well, the river, of course," I started.

"What did it sound like?"

"What do you mean?"

"Your eyes were closed. How do you know the sounds you heard were from the river?"

"Because it sounded like water!" I said.

"What does water sound like?"

"It sounds like . . ." I stopped, thinking about this for a minute. "I don't know. Water sounds like water."

"Which sounds like . . . ," Movado the Avocado pressed. "Give me a word."

I paused. "Slap."

"Good." Movado the Avocado's voice was gentle. "Slap. The slap of the water. Now. You've just created your very own imagery, May, which is what poetry is all about. Remember how much we talked about imagery last year?"

I nodded, although I had no idea how much we'd talked about anything last year. I hadn't been paying attention.

"Imagery is when you create pictures with words," Movado the Avocado said. "When you give your reader an image to think of, by saying something a certain way."

I tried to picture a hand made of water slapping the sides of the river. It worked. Sort of.

"What was another sound you heard?"

I thought back. "Birds."

"And what did the birds sound like?"

I hesitated.

"Just a word," Movado the Avocado encouraged. "Two, if you want."

"Lonely." I paused. "Afraid."

"Good," Movado the Avocado said. "Very good, May."

I liked hearing her say "Good" after something I'd said. During the year, practically the only thing she'd ever said to me was "Go downstairs to Principal Mola's office!" or "You have detention!" I wanted to hear more of the other stuff. It felt nice. I stretched out on a thin layer of moss and angled my hands underneath my head. "You do one," I said.

"A sound?" Movado the Avocado asked. "Or imagery?"

"Both." I stared up at the sky. Soft clouds, small as cotton balls, scuttled across the pale blue.

She looked out along the river. "Well, I heard the trees moving above me. The leaves rustling in the wind. And I guess I would describe them . . . well, maybe as fingers shaking their rings off."

I looked over at her. "That's good!"

She raised her eyebrows. "Yeah?"

"Yeah." I looked back up at the sky. "Real good." She didn't say anything, but I could tell she was pleased.

"This was a good place to bring us," I said. "To do this, I mean."

"I used to come down here with my best friend,"

Movado the Avocado said. "When we were younger."

"You mean the one you used to have the crazy sundaes with?" I asked. "Supercali?" I'd dubbed her with the new nickname just at that moment. The rest of the word—fun as it was to hear—was way too long to say.

Movado the Avocado chuckled. "The very one. We used to come right here—right to this spot—and look up at the clouds and pretend to be grown-ups."

"How old were you?"

"Oh, only about ten, I guess," she said. "Maybe eleven. But we had very elaborate games, I remember. I was always married to a guy who owned a Seven-Eleven and brought me a grape Slurpee every night. We had three children and a dog named Randy."

"Cherry Slurpees are better than grape," I said, realizing that I had no idea whether or not Movado the Avocado had a husband or children. "Do you have kids?"

"No, no," she said slowly. "No kids."

"Why not?"

She raised her eyebrows. "Why not? Well . . . I guess I never met someone I wanted to have them with."

I nodded. That was a pretty good answer. "So what kind of grown-up was Supercali?"

Movado the Avocado didn't say anything for a moment. When I turned, arching my neck so that I could see her, she held up one finger. "Hold on, I'm just thinking." There was a faraway look in her eyes. "Supercali was always married too. With kids. Yes, definitely kids. But she liked to pretend that they all lived far away, in a grass hut in Africa or a great big skyscraper in Japan. It was always someplace exotic."

"That's cool," I said. "Good for her. God, who wants to live in dumb old Sudbury the rest of their lives?" I bit my tongue, realizing that Movado the Avocado had been born, raised, and still lived in Sudbury. "I mean . . . you know, it's good to get out. Travel and stuff. See things."

"Yes," Movado the Avocado answered. "It certainly is."

"I have another imagery," I said, still staring up at the clouds.

"Go ahead."

"Cotton-ball clouds." I twisted my head so that I could look up at her again.

She was smiling. "Excellent, May. I think you've got it."

21

"Do you still go down there a lot?" Movado the Avocado and I were walking back to the school after our listening exercise down by the river. I was still trying to keep up, since she walked along just as briskly as she had before.

"No, not so much," she answered. We passed the electronic clock by the bank. The temperature said ninety-three degrees. I was surprised. It felt like it was at least a hundred.

"My, it's warm," Movado the Avocado said. She shifted her bag along her shoulder. It made a deep red dent in the soft skin along the collar.

"Here." I held out my purple notebook. "You can fan yourself with it." She took the notebook with a grateful smile and began waving it in front of her face. I could feel the little puffs of air as she moved it back and forth. Inside that notebook was one whole sheet filled with all different sorts of imagery I had come up with down by the river. The thought of it made me smile. Just a little.

"So are you and Supercali still best friends?" I asked.

"No." Movado the Avocado sighed deeply. "We lost touch a long time ago."

"How long?"

"High school."

"What happened in high school?"

"Oh, we had a falling-out." Movado the Avocado reached up and drew her finger down around the edge of her mouth. "You know, like girls do sometimes."

"What'd you do, steal her boyfriend or something?" I grinned.

Movado the Avocado did not grin. She didn't even smile a little. "No, it was nothing like that."

I didn't say anything more about it. Her tone had that finality to it that sort of killed every conversation. Plus, she was getting a little touchy. I figured it was better to just leave the subject alone. I waited a few minutes. Then: "Can I ask you another question?"

"Sure."

"Did you have a lot of friends in high school?"

Movado the Avocado looked over at me. "Not really."

No surprise there. "Was that by choice? Or were you, like, a mean person?"

She looked over at me again. A thin line of sweat was trickling down the side of her face. "Do you think I'm a mean person, May?"

Yes. Well, sort of. "I definitely *used* to," I said carefully. "But I mean, everyone in school thinks you're mean. Kinda."

"*Everyone* thinks I'm mean?" she repeated.

"Pretty much."

"Well, that's okay," she said. "I don't need my students to like me. You have to be firm when you're a teacher, May. Otherwise, your students will run all over you."

"Mr. Willowby is firm," I said. "And he's not mean." Mr. Willowby was my science teacher. He wore the same red shoes every day and was losing his hair. We laughed a lot in his class.

"Mr. Willowby is a very good teacher," Movado the Avocado concurred. "I've known him a long time. But he's a little soft."

"But the kids still listen to him."

"My students listen to me," Movado the Avocado said.

"It's different, though."

"How so?"

Because you yell and scream and kids are afraid to say stuff in your class because if they're wrong, you'll tear them apart and make them feel like a piece of dirt. And you don't give anyone a break. You don't care if people are trying their best. You just want them to be perfect. And anything less isn't good enough. It's not acceptable. "I don't know," I said.

She paused. "Can I ask you a question, then?"

"All right."

"Why do *you* think I'm mean?"

See above. I kicked another bottle cap on the sidewalk. Heineken. It scuttled along in front of me and then stopped. I kicked it again.

"May?"

"Will I get in trouble if I tell you?"

"No."

"You swear?"

Movado the Avocado held up her hand, palm out, like a Boy Scout.

Man, she was a dork.

So I told her. Everything that had run through my head a few seconds before all came out of me in one big rush. Every word. Except that I didn't yell it this time, the way I had before. I used a very calm, mature kind of voice. But I told her.

Movado the Avocado didn't say anything for a long

time after I finished. I walked along miserably beside her, sure that when we got back to the classroom she was going to make me stay late, or maybe even put me on manual labor again. Instead, as the front of the school loomed in front of us, she put a hand on my shoulder. "You go home now, May. There's only ten minutes left anyway. Go ahead. Enjoy the extra time. And have a good weekend."

"Are you sure?" I asked.

She nodded.

"Are you . . ." I hesitated. "You're not mad at me, are you? Because of everything I just said?"

She shook her head. "I'm not mad. Go on. I'll see you Monday."

I left. But just before I crossed the street, I turned around. Movado the Avocado was still standing there, watching me. I waved my hand.

She lifted hers, and then turned and went back into the building.

22

Friday night was just a long, empty stretch of time, since Olive's parents took her out of town to go visit her grandparents. She wouldn't be back until Saturday night, when she had invited me to sleep over, but I didn't know what I was going to do until then.

I played my harmonica for a while until I got bored, and fed Sherman some microwave popcorn, which he loved. His claws actually waved up and down when he saw a piece of popcorn in his cage, like I'd put a whole chocolate cake in there or something. He was funny. I watched him eat it—which took over half an hour, and then checked my MySpace page. Nothing. After our last argument, Brittany had sent out a mass e-mail to everyone, telling them to block me as their friend. Olive was the only one who sent me anything anymore on MySpace, and she was hardly ever on it.

I checked the Extreme Bodies section of the Guinness World Records webpage and found out that the loudest burp had been recorded at 107 decibels (which is the equivalent of standing next to a road drill), and that the furthest eyeball popper was completed by a woman in Turkey who was able to pop out her eyes almost a half inch from her face.

Gross, but kinda cool, too.

After a while, I turned off the computer and went into Gram's room. She was under the sheets, playing another game of solitaire. Purple half circles rested under her eyes, and her hair was gnarled on one side. I stretched out on her bed. Her room smelled musty, like old baby powder, and the blinds on her window were starting to collect dust.

"Don't you ever get bored of playing that game over and over?" I asked, propping myself up on one elbow.

"No," Gram answered.

"Do you want some tea?"

"No, thank you."

"Are you hungry?"

Gram shook her head.

"When did you eat last?"

"Lunch, I think. I had some tuna and crackers."

It was probably more like a sliver of tuna and one cracker.

"Do you mind if I turn on your TV?" I asked.

"Go ahead," Gram answered.

I picked up the remote, which was lying among the folds of sheets, and aimed it at the television. Next to me, Gram's hands slowed as an episode of *Little House on the Prairie* came on. I pointed the remote at the TV again, but Gram put her hand on my arm. A little whimpergrunt came out of her mouth.

"You want to watch this?" I asked, although I already knew the answer. It was one of Momma's favorite shows. Momma had seen every episode at least three times, watching them as a kid growing up, and then again as an adult. Just before she left, before things got really, really bad, she had lain in bed all day long and watched *Little House on the Prairie* reruns on TNT.

"This was your mother's favorite show," Gram said, as if I didn't already know. She smiled as Laura appeared on the screen. In her red prairie dress and tightly braided pigtails, she'd been Momma's favorite character. "Spunky little girl," Gram whispered as Laura began to argue with her father. "With a mind of her own."

I put the remote back down and lay up against Gram's arm for a while. Closed my eyes. She smelled faintly of sweat and buttered toast. Ahead of me, I could hear Laura still arguing with her pa. There was a new baby in the house and Laura didn't like it. The new baby was getting all the attention, and she missed her pa. "I hate my baby brother!" Laura finally shouted, before running out of their little house. "I wish he'd never been born!"

I didn't open my eyes again until the familiar theme song signaling the end of the show began to play. Gram sniffed. It was a soupy sound, clogged with tears. I reached over and grabbed a pink Kleenex off her night table. She took it without a word and pressed it under her nose. I leaned in closer, held her tight.

"I wish . . . ," Gram said. Her words were muffled against the Kleenex.

I waited, but she didn't say any more. I hoped she was going to say something about me. *I wish you could stay home with me all the time, May. I wish I could go back to the way I was before and make breakfast for you again.* "You wish what, Gram?"

She shook her head. Pressed the Kleenex harder against her lips. Thin blue veins, like rivers drawn on a map, threaded their way along the tops of her hands. Her nails needed to be filed.

"What, Gram?"

"I wish I'd done better," she cried. "I wish I could go

back and do it again. Do it differently somehow. Make her happier this time."

Her. She meant Momma. I bit my lip. Swallowed over two parallel lines of pain stitched along the inside of my throat.

"Well, you can't," I said, getting up. "No one can, Gram. It's impossible."

I made a move toward the foot of her bed, watching her out of the corner of my eye. *Ask me to stay, Gram. Ask me to sit back down and hold you again.*

Instead she pushed the pink Kleenex against her eyes and shook her head.

I left, shutting the door carefully behind me, and walked back into my room.

23

I slept in late on Saturday. The sun streamed through my room with yellow fingers, nudging me awake. I reached for my phone. One message, from Olive: WE'LL BE HOME BY 6. PICK U UP FOR SLEEPOVER?

YES! I texted back. GET ME OUT OF HERE!

Olive's response was a smiley face.

Dad was already gone for work. Gram was still sleeping. The sun shone through the windows, bright as glass. I poured myself a bowl of Cocoa Krispies and ate at the kitchen table. But it tasted too sweet for some reason, and I dumped the rest down the sink. I went back into my room. Opened my journal notebook.

Prompt #3: Describe yourself using ten adjectives in alphabetical order. I snorted. Back in April, when this prompt had been on Movado the Avocado's blackboard, I had written curse words after the first ten letters of the alphabet. When she'd come across it, after collecting our journals at the end of the year for grading, she'd drawn a huge red *X* over the whole thing. Immediately.

Now I sat down. Made a list of the first ten letters of the alphabet. Looked out the window. Nibbled on the end of my pencil eraser.

A: angry

B: bad

C: care (as in don't)

D: deserted

E: empty

F: funny (sometimes)

G: grouchy

H: hurt

I: icky

J: jumbled

That was me in a nutshell, I thought, looking over the words again. And then, because a slow pain was starting to form in the center of my chest, I turned the page.

Prompt #4: What is your earliest memory? Try to describe it in two or more paragraphs.

A thrumming sensation began to make its way through my fingertips as I walked over to my dresser. The only other time I'd done this was right after I knew Momma was gone, after it had started to sink in that she wasn't coming back. I'd been afraid, for some reason, that I would forget what she looked like. Afterward, I'd shut the drawer again and run out of my room.

Now I opened the bottom drawer, reached into the very back, all the way under an old New York Knicks sweatshirt Dad had given me, and pulled out the photograph of Momma. It was unframed, and the upper left-hand corner was bent over just a little. I pushed it back with my thumb, and then ran my fingers lightly over the glossy middle, tracing the outline of Momma's nose, the line of hair that trailed down her back like inky water, the smooth curve of her neck. I'd taken this photo when I was about eight years old, after finding a disposable camera at the bottom of Momma's beach bag. She'd been doing dishes at the sink, swinging her hips back and forth to a song coming out of the kitchen radio.

"Momma!" I'd said.

She looked over her shoulder, eyebrows up, expectant.

I gasped happily as her image appeared through the tiny square lens. "Say cheese!" I yelled.

Her mouth broke into a grin, deepening the dimple in her cheek.

I pushed the button.

She looked so happy, I thought now. She always looked happy when someone caught her unaware, as if for a split second, before she had a chance to think about it, the little-girl joy that Gram had seen, the cartwheel-happiness that hid somewhere inside of her, peeked its head out again. It was the rest of the time—when she did think, when she spent all that time brooding—that it disappeared. And the rest of the time, unfortunately, had become most of the time.

But there had been a few of those unaware moments.

And now, as I remembered one, I walked back over and sat down at my desk.

My earliest memory is of being taken out of my crib by my mother. I was crying. I think my teeth hurt. It was dark out. She carried me into the kitchen, opened the refrigerator, and took out an orange. I held on to her hair the way I always did, because it was long and it was always in the way. Momma set me on the counter while she cut *the orange into slices. I was still crying, but softer now, because Momma was there and she smelled like toothpaste and peaches.*

She gave me a piece of orange to suck on. It was cold and sweet. It made my teeth feel better. Momma took a slice of orange too. She put it in her mouth and poked me in the shoulder. When I looked at her, her whole mouth was just one wide smooth band of orange. No teeth at all. I laughed. She laughed too.

I stopped writing.

Put my head down on my notebook.

Stayed that way for a long, long time without moving.

24

Olive's parents picked me up at six o'clock, just as she said they would. Dad was home by then, since he only worked half days on Saturday, and had even started making something to eat by the time I left. Pasta, I think, since there was a pot of water on the stove. He liked it plain, without the sauce, sprinkled with a little butter and salt. Maybe he'd get Gram to eat some.

I'd always felt a little weird in front of Olive's parents, maybe because Olive and I are so different, but ever since Momma left, I actually got nervous around them. Like my hands would sweat and I started to itch all over, that kind of nervous. It wasn't like they didn't know about Momma; everyone in Sudbury knew everything about everyone else, for better or for worse. But Olive's mother had a way now—a life coach sort of way, I guess—of looking at me with these new puppy-dog eyes that made me want to reach out and whack her.

Tonight, though, neither of Olive's parents seemed particularly interested in me. In fact, as I slid into the back of their Range Rover, Mrs. Masters barely turned her head. "Hello, May," she said stiffly, and then stared back out the window.

I glanced over at Olive, who pointed at the back of her father's head. *She's mad at him,* she mouthed. *They're arguing.*

I still don't know why this fact made me feel a little warm inside. Maybe it was because I'd always envied Olive for having two seemingly perfect parents. Or maybe it was just because both of them—her mom, especially—seemed just the tiniest bit more real now that I knew they *could* get mad.

We ordered pizza for dinner—half plain for Mrs. Masters, the other half loaded with pepperoni and mushrooms for Olive, me, and Mr. Masters. Olive and I brought our pizza and soda up to her room and watched a movie while we ate. Right in the middle of the movie (which was really boring), I drank a second soda superfast—without even stopping for a breath—and then let out a gigantic burp. It was so loud that my lips actually quivered when it came out. Olive was horrified, until she accidentally let out a burp of her own. It was not even an eighth of the size of my burp, but I laughed so hard my stomach hurt. Then Olive laughed, and right in the middle of laughing, she let out another one! By then I couldn't breathe, and I was so full that I thought I might actually wet my pants, so I ran into the bathroom.

We stayed up until one o'clock, eating buttered popcorn and playing a Super Uno marathon. Olive won in a sudden-death round. I brushed my teeth once more, since a few popcorn kernels had gotten lodged in the back of my teeth, and then we coated our faces with a bright blue mud mask that Olive's mom had given her. The best part about the mud mask was the faces we made when it dried; the mud split and cracked over our skin like pieces of dried desert clay. It looked so cool.

By the time we finally turned off the lights and pulled Olive's blue comforter up over us, it was almost two in the morning. I was drowsy with happiness. At times like this, it felt like I could get through anything—as long as Olive was there next to me.

25

"So what do you think Movado'll make you do tomorrow?" Olive and I were dressing the next morning. Mrs. Masters was downstairs, making bacon and pancakes for breakfast. It was almost ten.

I shrugged, pulling on my jeans. I had a headache, probably from all the junk we'd eaten last night, and I hadn't slept well, thanks to Olive's incessant snoring. "Who knows? Some other dumb thing, probably."

"Dumb?" Olive repeated. "You think the stuff she's doing with you is dumb?"

Truthfully, I didn't know what to think of the things Movado the Avocado had been doing with me. Breakfast at Sweet Treet, a lesson in imagery down by the river. Who knew what was next? But I felt embarrassed talking about it, for some reason—even with Olive. Movado the Avocado's suggestions were definitely original; I would give her that. But they also made me feel like I was some kind of special case. Like I couldn't be treated just like any other student. I knew I wasn't in the same smarts league as Olive, but I didn't want to be thought of as disadvantaged, either.

"Yeah, I think it's dumb," I said now. "I mean, the lady's weird, Olive. There's no getting around it. She's *weird*."

"What's weird about taking you places?" Olive asked. "I think it's great. I wish I had a teacher like that."

"Well, I wish you could switch places with me, then. 'Cause I hate it. First I have to work my butt off all morning painting her room, then she drags me to all these freaky places."

"You complain a lot, you know that?" Olive brushed her long hair with smooth, even strokes.

I glanced over at her. "Maybe that's because I have stuff to complain about."

"Complaining is just a waste of time," Olive said, fastening a barrette over one ear. "It doesn't get you anywhere."

"Well, you try living my life sometime." I threw my dirty clothes into my backpack, as if I was shoving down the annoyance that was starting to creep up too. "And then you see if you feel like you want to complain."

Olive turned, both barrettes in her hair now. "But see, that's just it, May. Complaining just—"

"Oh, would you just *stop*?" The loudness of my voice startled even me.

Olive stared at me, wide eyed.

"I mean it, Olive. It's . . . it's like you *want* to see me suffer! Like I haven't been through enough this last year!"

"I don't want to see you suffer," Olive said quietly.

"Then why do you keep nagging me about this whole situation?" I mimicked her voice, raising mine to a nasally falsetto. "Just do it, May. Attitude is everything. There's no use complaining. It'll be over soon. You do something like that, you gotta face the consequences."

"Because you *do*." Olive's face had taken on that absolute quality, a set-in-stone look that appeared when she was one hundred percent sure of herself about something. It annoyed me to no end. It was also something I envied. I'd never been one hundred percent sure about anything in my whole life. "That's just the way it goes, May. I mean, that's what it means to be a decent person. You dish it out, you gotta take it. No matter how much stuff you've already been through. And complaining about it isn't going to help anything either. Actually, it just makes it worse."

I shook my head. "Now you sound like Principal Mola *and* your mother. You know that? You sound like a first-class dork, just like them. You don't know anything."

It was as if someone had pressed a switch inside my head. I was off to the races, exactly the way I'd been during that last horrible showdown with Brittany.

"You don't have to insult my mother," Olive said quietly.

"I wouldn't have to if you didn't make it so easy. Get your own brain, Olive, instead of borrowing hers all the time. And then use it."

Olive looked so hurt when I said that that I almost reached out and hugged her. *OhmyGodI'msorryIdidn'tmean itOliveIswearIdidn'tpleasedon'thateme.* But another part of me didn't care that she felt bad. And so I stepped over her chair instead, which for some reason was lying on its side, and walked out her bedroom door. "I'm leaving!"

"Go ahead," I heard Olive say. "Go home and feel sorry for yourself some more."

I stopped on the middle step. Clenched the banister until my whole fist ached. I knew if I went back upstairs and got in Olive's face, I would do something that would destroy our friendship forever, like when I'd shoved Brittany out of the way last year, almost knocking her over. And if I did that, I would be left with no one.

"Aaaaggggghhhh!" I screamed instead. And then I said something so mean and horrible that even if someone was torturing me right now, I probably wouldn't be able to bring

myself to say it again. When the last of it had made its way out of my mouth, I stood there for a split second, clutching the stair railing and panting like a dog.

Olive did not come out of her room.

There was no sign of Mrs. Masters, either. She was still in the kitchen, I guessed, cooking up breakfast. Mr. Masters was still sleeping.

I ran.

26

I raced the whole six blocks home from Olive's, as if her parents were chasing me or something. Which they weren't, of course. I couldn't be sure if Mrs. Masters had actually heard the horrible thing I said on the stairs, but I was almost positive that once she found me gone so abruptly, she would get Olive to talk about it. Life coaches were big on things like talking about your feelings. Olive had told me that. And once that happened, once Olive told her mother what I'd said and how rude I'd been, I'd probably be banned from their house forever.

I tried not to think about it as I slipped back inside the apartment. Dad was still asleep on the couch—he would be there until at least noon, since he didn't have to work at all on Sundays—and I could hear Gram snoring faintly in her room. Dad's red and yellow afghan was half on the floor; I stopped on my way in to my room, and covered him back up with it. He was in his T-shirt and jeans; his work boots were in a heap in the corner. I could smell the stale scent of beer around him, the rancid stench of old cigarettes. Ugh.

I lay on my bed for a long time and tried to go back to sleep. I was worn out all over again from the run home, and now my legs ached too. But every time I closed my eyes, I just saw Olive's face when I started yelling at her. I stared up at the ceiling. *Idon'tcareIdon'tcareIdon'tcare Idon'tcareIdon'tcareIdon'tcare.* And then, because that wasn't helping either, I pulled my pillow over my head, blocking out the light and sound from the window outside.

After a while, I heard Dad stirring out in the living room. The TV went on, followed by the crack and hiss of a can opening. Dad had the same routine every Sunday: He watched old Western movies on TV until it got dark out, and ate chips and soda until dinnertime, when he ordered us a pizza, or maybe some Chinese takeout. Then he went back to sleep.

I hardly ever hung around with Dad on Sundays. Usually I was out doing something with Olive. However, now that the possibility of ever talking to her again was probably nonexistent, and the thought of spending one more second in my room made me want to scream, I found myself standing on the edge of the living room rug, deliberating whether or not I should sit down and watch TV with him. We still hadn't talked—not since the grilled-cheese incident—but that wasn't unusual these days either. Quickly, before I changed my mind, I sat down—all the way at the other end of the couch—and curled my feet up under me.

On TV, two cowboys were sitting on their horses, talking to each other. The night sky was pitch-black, but a fire snapped and crackled in front of them, making weird shadows across their faces. Dad loved his old cowboy movies. Watching them was what had made him want to learn the harmonica. Sometimes I watched them with him. Mostly, though, I fell asleep. Dad's cowboys spent too much time talking in deep, boring voices.

"Hey," Dad said after a minute, without taking his eyes off the TV.

"Hey."

His bare feet were stretched out in front of him, resting on the small glass table in between the couch and the TV. Dad's toes were long and bony, and covered with little tufts of black hair. Yuck. Bare feet gave me the willies. He was eating out of a big bag of potato chips, shoving three or four chips at a time into his mouth and crunching loudly. He held the bag out in my direction.

I took a few chips and placed them in my palm. Rippled, thick cut. My favorite. I ate them slowly, one ridge at a time. "Did you go shopping?" I asked.

"Just got a few things last night on my way home from work. Soda, some chips. Tea for Gram. More Cocoa Krispies." He dug his hand into his front pocket and pulled out a ten-dollar bill. "Had a little extra, actually. Keep it."

I could feel a little lump in my throat. The last thing I had said to him before today was that I hated him. Three times, if I remembered correctly. Maybe even four. "Um . . . thanks," I said softly.

He crossed his feet, one ankle over the other. The hem of his blue jeans was ripped. "How you been?" he asked, still watching the TV. "Gram says you've been in your room since this morning. I thought you were over at Olive's. Where is she?"

Just hearing her name hurt. "She's . . . home, I guess. With her parents."

"How was the sleepover?"

I shrugged. "Good."

Dad nodded, as if he understood perfectly. He hadn't shaved yet, and the bristle along the sides of his face was dark. I hated it when he didn't shave. It made him look like a bum. "How's the summer school going?" he asked.

"Okay."

Finally he turned, looking at me full in the face. He had bags under his eyes and deep lines around the corners of them. He'd been working double shifts on the road for the last six months, to try to make more money. I'd never seen him look so tired.

"Yeah?" he asked. "Really?"

I nodded. "It's not how I want to spend my summer, but I'm doing it."

Dad uncrossed his feet. "Well, you'd better keep doing it. And do it with a smile on your face too. Because if I hear about you getting into one more incident up at that school, I'm telling you right now, May—"

"Why do you have to do this?" I tossed my chips back into the bag. "I tell you I'm doing it, which I *am*, and then you have to go and rub it in my face by saying stuff like that."

"Stuff like what?" Dad asked loudly.

"Like 'You'd *better* do it,' and 'Do it with a smile on your face.' That stuff. You always have to make me feel worse about everything. Like things aren't bad enough already."

Dad sat up a little and ran a hand through his thick hair. "You know what, May? I'm getting just a little bit sick and tired of you whining about your life all the time, you know that? You're the one who goes and gets yourself into all this trouble, and then you spend the rest of the time crying about how to get yourself out of it."

"I'm not crying about getting myself out of it!" I shouted. "I'm in *summer* school, okay, Dad? I'm fixing my mistake! Okay? So just lay off!"

He stood up. Got the index finger out and moved it in dangerously close to my face. "You watch how you talk to me. I don't care how much you dislike me right now, but I am still your father."

"Then act like one!" I screamed.

"You go to your room!" he yelled.

"Fine!"

I slammed my door.

Dad turned up the volume on the TV.

For the rest of the afternoon and into the evening, the galloping sound of cowboy music blared through the apartment. I lay on my bed for a while until I thought I might kick the wall in, and then I took Sherman out of his cage. It took him about an hour and a half to walk up and down the length of my arm. By the time he got to my elbow again, I lost interest and put him back in. Around nine o'clock, I heard the sound of the front door opening and then shutting again. I knew exactly where Dad was going. The Wooden Nickel was just around the corner. We wouldn't see him again until the small, barely lit hours of the morning.

I took my shoe off and threw it across the room.

27

There was a gigantic can of paint primer sitting next to Movado the Avocado's desk on Monday morning. There were also two paintbrushes—one a large roller, the other a smaller regular brush—several masks like doctors wore when they performed surgery, a ladder, a square tin paint pan, and a gigantic white smock.

"All yours," Movado the Avocado said as I surveyed the items. "Time to get to work. It's paintin' time!"

Truth be told, I was glad I had to paint. The last thing in the world I wanted to do right then was talk. To anyone. I'd woken up in the middle of the night and crept out to the living room to look for Dad, but the couch was still empty. I'd gone into Gram's room and lay down next to her, but I didn't sleep at all, not even when I heard the front door open at two thirty in the morning.

I sat up and listened as Dad stumbled into the bathroom and then collapsed on the couch. I lay very still until I heard the heavy fluttering of his snores, and then I still didn't move. Finally, when the first light started to bleed through Gram's blinds, fragile and pale as eggshells, I got up and took a shower. I put some mashed banana in Sherman's cage, refilled his water dish, and tiptoed out of the apartment.

Now I shoved my arms through the arms of the smock and buttoned it up. I snapped the surgery mask over my face and dipped the large roller brush into the tin container filled with paint. The primer was a dull white color. This was going to be *really* fun. It'd be like painting into oblivion. And the ceiling was at least a foot above my head. How was I supposed to reach up there? She didn't expect me to get up on that ladder.

Did she?

"The ladder is right over there," Movado the Avocado said, as if reading my mind. "Let me know when you're ready to set it up and I'll help you."

I grunted my thanks.

"How was your weekend?" Movado the Avocado asked, as I began the first strokes. "Did you do anything interesting?"

I shook my head and concentrated on moving the roller in a straight line. After the fiasco with the blue tape, I didn't want to take any chances. The roller made a soft sucking sound as it moved over the wall, and the acrid smell of paint drifted in behind my mask. Just to be polite then, and since she had asked first, I said, "Did you?"

"Actually, I did!" Movado the Avocado said brightly.

I rolled my eyes, glad that she couldn't see me. It figured that on the day I wanted some peace and quiet, Movado the Avocado was all fired up. Life always worked like that. At odds with itself. It never went in a straight line. Never, ever, ever.

"I saw a marvelous movie on Friday night, and then I went to an all-day craft fair over at the college on Saturday."

Whoop-de-friggin-do. I turned back around and kept painting. My arm was already starting to ache.

"Have you ever been to a craft fair, May?" Movado the Avocado asked. I shook my head. "They're fun!" she said. "Really! If you like crafts, of course." She picked up a yellow yarn box that covered the tissues on her desk. "I bought this at a fair. I love crafts. I can't do any of them, but I love looking at them. And shopping for them. There's one fair that East Sudbury holds every year. . . ."

I tuned her out right about then. She kept going, oblivious to the fact that I was far, far away from any craft-fair land she had just gone back to. I wondered what Olive was doing, what kind of things she was thinking. Probably how being friends with me was one of the worst mistakes of her life and that now that she had seen the light, she was going to run as fast as she could in the opposite direction. I hadn't gotten a single text from her yesterday—or today. I wondered how Gram was doing back home, if she'd gotten up yet. And Dad. Would he get up in time to get to work? I knew he'd been reprimanded before for being late. He'd yelled about it during one of our fights. Like it was my fault or something.

"My sister came with me," Movado the Avocado said suddenly. "She loves crafts too."

I turned around. "You have a sister?"

She smiled and nodded.

"Here?" I asked. "In Sudbury?"

"The one and only."

I turned back around and slid the roller up the wall again. For some reason, I'd always thought of Movado the Avocado as an only child. Like me. She didn't seem like the type to have a sister, just like she didn't seem the type to have a husband. Or even friends, for that matter.

"You don't have any brothers or sisters, do you, May?" she asked.

"Nope." I shook my head. "Just me."

"I didn't think so."

Something inside prickled a little when she said that. Did *I* seem like the type of person who was an only child? Or did she mean that she couldn't imagine any more like me coming down the line? "Yup," I heard myself saying, as if I needed to elaborate. "My mother had a hard time having just me. She had a bad back. My dad said the delivery and everything was pretty difficult. Anyway, that was it for her."

Movado the Avocado was quiet. "Well, I'm sure she was thrilled to have you."

I shrugged. "I guess." And then, because I wanted to steer the conversation far away from Momma, I said, "Do you hang out a lot with your sister?"

"Hmm . . . not really," Movado the Avocado answered.

"Why not?"

Movado the Avocado placed the yellow yarn box back over the top of her tissues. "We're . . . very different people." She spoke slowly, as if she was choosing her words. "We don't always see things eye-to-eye."

"You mean you fight a lot."

She didn't answer.

I turned around. "Do you fight a lot?"

She shrugged and then gave a sort of half nod. "Well, we argue. Sometimes. You know, like siblings do."

"Is she older than you or younger?" I asked.

"Younger," Movado the Avocado said. "Much younger, actually."

"She probably thinks you're too bossy."

Movado the Avocado gave a little gruntlaugh. "She says that quite a bit, as a matter of fact."

I bet she does. "No one likes bossy people," I said.

"Hmm," Movado the Avocado murmured. "Maybe not."

28

I pressed the lid of the primer paint down tightly and watched Movado the Avocado out of the corner of my eye. She hadn't moved from her desk yet and her purse was still slung over the back of her chair. I didn't expect her to take me out *every* day during summer school. But it was kind of nice when she did. And I found myself looking forward to it just the tiniest little bit. I folded the smock neatly and put it on top of the primer. Then I went to the girls' bathroom to wash out the paintbrushes.

It was weird being inside the bathroom with no one else around. When I dumped the paint tin into one of the sinks, it actually echoed throughout the pink tiled walls. When school was in session, someone was always sneaking a cigarette in the last stall, or there was a small gathering in front of the mirror. The bathroom mobs only visited between classes, when girls felt the overwhelming need to brush their hair out for the seventeenth time or reapply their eyeliner before biology. My visits to the bathroom happened *during* class, when only the occasional emergency visitor was in a stall, or no one at all. That was when I would whip out my purple permanent marker and go to work on the walls.

I ran my hand over the walls. They were smooth and clean now. Pete had done a good job painting over all the garbage written on them. I leaned in. He must have done two coats, maybe even a primer layer first. You couldn't see anything, not even the dirty knock-knock jokes next to the mirror. I felt a twinge inside as I thought about how much work he'd had to do—partly because of me.

When I got back to Movado the Avocado's room, she was standing next to her desk. Her purse was slung over one shoulder. I tried not to smile.

"You okay with going out again?" she asked.

"Yeah," I said casually. "Sure."

I ran for my poetry notebook.

This time, we went to the YMCA. I thought it was a pretty weird destination, but by now, I'd learned not to ask so many questions. The Sudbury YMCA was in a large brick building about a half mile from the school. I'd gone to the day care when I was little for a few days a week. The teacher had been awful, putting me in the corner when I wouldn't stop crying, and then ignoring me for the rest of the morning. Eventually I'd fall asleep. When Momma came to get me, the lady would tell her I'd slept the whole time.

I'd never been to any other part of the YMCA except that day-care room, and so when Movado the Avocado led me to a small gymnasium in the back of the building, I looked at her like she was crazy.

"I can't play basketball," I said.

She laughed. "Neither can I. Look."

The gymnasium was packed with all kinds of gymnastic equipment. A set of uneven bars, streaked with chalk, had been set up near the door. A high balance beam and a smaller, lower one were arranged in the middle, side by side. Red floor mats the size of our whole apartment took up the right-hand side, and a vault with a path of blue mats spread out in front of it lined the left wall. Two girls dressed in black leotards stood next to the high beam, talking. Another girl readied herself in front of the vault. Still another began rubbing the uneven bars down with powdered chalk. It flew out from between her hands like fairy dust. An older woman wearing a blue track suit with white lines on the sides clapped her hands and walked around. "Let's go, girls!" she said loudly. Her voice echoed through the big room. "Time to get to work."

"I come here sometimes to watch them practice," Movado the Avocado said, nodding as one of the girls by the beam waved at her. "I love to see the things they can do." I followed her toward a set of bleacher benches without taking my eyes off the girl standing by the vault. She was up on her tiptoes, her upper body clenched tight, her fists at her side. A blond ponytail sprouted out of the back of her head, and her brow was furrowed with concentration. She looked so fierce! And so determined! I held my breath as she gave a little skip and then started running down the path of blue mats toward the springboard. Her feet made a thundering sound as she picked up speed, and her elbows scissored tightly against her sides.

"Hoe. Lee. Cow." The words came out of my mouth in tandem with the girl's aerial movements above the vault. Her whole body arched upward and then spun around through the air. It was as if she floated there for a second, suspended somehow against the chalk-filled atmosphere—before she crashed back down again.

Her landing was not nearly as pretty. She fell back on both hands, and then toppled over on her side.

"Whoa!" I stood up. "Is she hurt?"

The coach, who had been standing at the other end of the blue mats, knelt down next to the girl. Slowly, the fallen girl sat up. She pushed a strand of hair off her forehead and shook her head. The coach said something softly to her and patted her on the back. The girl on the mat laughed. Stood up. Walked back to the other end of the blue mats to do it again.

I was mesmerized. An hour passed as Movado the Avocado and I sat in the gymnasium and watched the girls practice. We didn't say a word, except to point out what one of the girls was doing over there, or *ohmygoshlook!* at that girl over here. The gymnasts were lithe and strong at the same time, fearless and agile as cats. They flipped over the narrow expanse of beam as if it were a kitchen table instead of the width of a human hand. The muscles in their legs strained as they flew under the uneven bars, catching the top one with their hands and barely skimming the bottom one with their pointed feet. And when they tumbled, when they ran across the wide red mats and flung themselves up into the air and rotated neatly—wildly!—before coming back down again—upright! on their feet!—I pressed my fingers against my lips and held my breath.

They fell a lot too. One of them, who was in the middle of a tumbling run, cried out when she slipped, and then sat there for a while on the sidelines with a bag of ice on her ankle. But after a while she went back out. She didn't run quite as fast this time, and she completed only one flip instead of two, but the coach nodded and clapped, and the girl looked happy. I couldn't believe it. If I had hurt myself badly enough to need ice on my ankle, you wouldn't see me running back out there. Even if it was just half an effort. No sir. I'd be sitting on my keister, trying to catch my breath. Enjoying a much-needed break.

After a while, Movado the Avocado touched my shoulder. "C'mon," she said, standing up. "We have to go."

"Go where?" I tried not to sound annoyed.

"We still have work to do, May," she said, making her way toward the outside door of the gym. "Come on, now. This was just the first half of the lesson."

29

We walked the half mile back to school. No dice on leaving early this time, I thought, as we opened the front doors of the school again and climbed the steps. Movado the Avocado was all excited about something too, which was making me a little edgy. I sighed as she sat down across from me and folded her hands. Her eyes were unnervingly bright. I wondered briefly what Olive was doing.

"Now. Let's discuss that poem that got us into this whole mess to begin with," she said.

"The raisin one?"

"The raisin one." Movado the Avocado slid a sheet of paper onto my desk and picked up another one. It was a copy of the poem. "The title is 'Harlem.' It was written by

Mr. Langston Hughes. We did an extensive background lesson regarding Mr. Hughes, May. Do you remember any of it?"

"No."

"Nothing at all?"

"No."

Movado the Avocado cocked her head. "Are you going to be difficult now?"

"I *hate* poetry."

"That's what you said about writing."

"Poetry's worse."

"Why?"

"I don't know! It just is. It's boring, it doesn't make sense, it uses too many big words. . . ." I shrugged. "You want me to keep going?"

"I want you to read this poem aloud," Movado the Avocado said, tapping her paper. "Read 'Harlem' aloud to me, May."

I sat up a little. "'What happens to a dream deferred?'"

I stopped. "See? Right there. I have no idea what the word 'deferred' means. I've never heard of that word in my life." I pushed the paper away.

"It means delayed," Movado the Avocado said. "When something has to be put off. Done later." She pushed the paper back in front of me. "Read."

"What happens to a dream deferred?
Does it dry up
Like a raisin in the sun?
Or fester like a sore—
And then run?"

I looked up. "Fester?"

"It means to get infected," Movado the Avocado said. "When a sore gets all runny and swollen because it hasn't been treated properly."

"Oh." I wrinkled my nose. "Gross."

"Keep going."

"Does it stink like rotten meat?
Or crust and sugar over—
Like a syrupy sweet?

Maybe it just sags
like a heavy load.

Or does it explode?"

I looked up. "It just . . . it makes no sense. At all. That's exactly what I'm talking about."

"Why doesn't it make sense?"

"What do you mean, why doesn't it make sense? It just doesn't!"

"Think about it, May. What's Mr. Hughes talking about?"

"No idea."

"You do have an idea. I just explained the words you didn't understand. Now, what's he talking about?"

I looked back down at the paper. Read the first line again. "Dreams that have to wait," I said. "I guess."

"Exactly," Movado the Avocado said.

I felt something swell a little inside my chest.

"What does Mr. Hughes think happens to dreams that have to be put off? What does he tell us?"

I looked back down at the poem. "They shrivel up or something. Or get infected and gooey and stuff."

"Keep going."

"They smell bad." I looked up. "Come on. How can a *dream* smell bad?"

"It's imagery again, May," Movado the Avocado said. "Mr. Hughes is comparing an unfulfilled dream to all these different things: a raisin in the sun, stinking meat, a split-open candy."

"'Crust and sugar over like a syrupy sweet,'" I said. "Maybe he was thinking of one of those cough drops that have a liquid center. You know what I'm talking about?

Maybe a dream that has to wait is like one of those cough drops that someone steps on, and it just lays there, with all the stuff inside dribbling out and getting all crusty and stuff."

Movado the Avocado looked at me. "Write that down," she said. "Just the way you said it."

"About the cough drop?"

She nodded. "About the cough drop. Write it, May. Write it down."

I wrote it down.

"Now," Movado the Avocado said. "I want you to think about those girls we just watched at the gym. If Mr. Hughes here has compared a deferred dream to a crusty, dribbly cough drop thingy, what do you think those girls would compare losing the ability to run and flip and twist like that to?"

"You mean what would it be like if they could never do that stuff again?"

"Maybe they could," Movado the Avocado said. "But they wouldn't know when. Or if. They'd have to wait. Put off doing their favorite thing in the world. Indefinitely."

I tried to think. Throughout the whole practice, the girls' faces were shiny with exhilaration. Excitement. Even when they fell. Maybe it was from the possibility of making the next move perfect. Or the one after that. "It'd be awful," I said. "Terrible."

"Those are feelings," Movado the Avocado said. "Remember, we're talking about images here. Things that paint a picture to show the feeling. Can you try to give me some words that would represent what those girls might feel if someone told them they had to stop doing gymnastics?"

"Sad." I stopped myself. "No, wait, that's a feeling."

"Try again," Movado the Avocado said. "What do you think it would feel like? Give me a picture, May."

I closed my eyes. "It would be like standing in an apartment full of people." My voice got real quiet for some reason. "And not just any people. Not strangers. People you know. People you love. People who make you laugh and say all the right things to you when you're sad." I started picking at my thumb. "Except that now, all these people are in their rooms, with the doors closed. And no one comes out. And you can't get in. Ever." I opened my eyes. "That's what I think it would feel like."

Movado the Avocado stared at me for a second.

"What?" I asked.

She blinked. "Nothing. Sometimes, May, you just surprise the bejesus out of me."

Now I blinked. "Bejesus?" I repeated. "What the heck does bejesus mean? Is that even a word?"

She laughed. "It's just a word we old people use." Her face got solemn again. "I want you to try to write that down, May, in your journal tonight. What you just told me about the rooms and not being able to get in. See if any more comes." She nodded. "That's your homework. Along with your journal prompts."

"You want me to do *all* of that?" I asked. "The imagery thing, plus two journal prompts?"

She nodded. "I think you can handle it."

I sighed. "So are we done now? I can go?"

Movado the Avocado grinned a little. "You can go."

I scooped up my notebooks and headed for the door.

"May?"

"Yeah?" I turned around.

"That time in class, when you said I laughed at you about this poem?"

I bit the inside of my cheek.

"Do you remember what it was you said?"

I remembered perfectly. It had been one of those rare days when I hadn't exactly felt like trying, and I *definitely* didn't care one way or the other, but I'd been listening with half an ear anyway. Movado the Avocado had read 'Harlem' three times aloud to the class, and now she was pacing up and down the length of the room, shouting out questions. There were a few timid answers, but most of the students just stared down at the poem. "Why do you think Mr. Hughes asks so many questions in this poem?" she'd asked at one point. I raised my hand.

Movado the Avocado's eyebrows shot up. It was probably the first time all year I'd volunteered for real in class. "May?"

"Because he doesn't know the answer," I'd said.

It hadn't really been a laugh. It was more like a *ppph-hhttt* sound she made with her lips. "He doesn't *know* the answer?" she repeated. "How could the author of a poem not know the answer to his own question?"

I'd shut down, right then and there, as the tips of my ears burned hot. My brain started moving at the speed of light, trying to figure out a way to humiliate her the same way she'd just humiliated me. A few minutes later, after I'd come up with the whole avocado drawing plan, I felt better.

"No," I said now, stepping on the toe of my shoe. "I can't really remember anymore what I said."

Something flickered across Movado the Avocado's face. "You're sure?"

I nodded. For some reason, that revenge feeling I'd had toward her before wasn't really there anymore. Or at least it wasn't as strong. "See you tomorrow," I said.

"Okay." She gave me a little wave with her hand. "See you tomorrow, then, May."

30

Gram was looking through an old photo album when I came in, turning the crinkly pages carefully as she peered at each one.

"Hey," I said, tapping on her door frame. "How you doing?"

She didn't look up. "All right."

"You need anything?"

She shook her head.

"No tea?"

"No, dear."

"Toast?"

She patted the side of her bed. I closed my eyes. "Sit with me, May. Look at this."

I walked over and sat down on the side of the bed. The

album pages were filled with pictures of Momma when she was a little girl, her long raven hair spilling down her back, a pair of buck teeth jutting out of the front of her mouth. I couldn't do another story. Not today. Not like this. "I have a lot of homework, Gram. I'm sorry."

Without looking up from the picture of Momma, she nodded her head. I leaned over quickly, dropped a kiss on top of her wispy hair, and walked back out.

And then I walked back in.

Gram looked up.

"Do you think I feel sorry for myself?" I blurted out.

"I don't know," Gram answered slowly. "Do you?"

"I mean . . . about what happened. With Momma . . . and everything."

Gram didn't say anything right away. And for a split, stricken second, I thought maybe she was going to say yes. But she didn't. "I think you should go easy on yourself when it comes to feeling anything about your momma," she said. "If you want to feel sorry for yourself, then feel sorry for yourself. If you want to feel mad, then feel mad. If you don't want to feel anything, then don't feel anything."

I couldn't see her clearly through the film of tears that had clouded my eyes. I blinked. "Is that . . . sorta . . . how you're doing it?"

She nodded, steadying a palm against the photo album.

"Okay," I whispered. "Thanks, Gram."

"It'll be okay, May," Gram said. "It will."

I nodded.

Shut her door.

I didn't believe her.

31

It had been more than twenty-four hours since the fight between Olive and me. I hadn't gotten a single text message from her, and there were no messages on MySpace. I checked all my deleted messages twice, just in case I had erased one from her, but there was nothing there. I knew I was the one who needed to call first, that I was the one who had messed up. But I couldn't do it, for some reason. Something inside just wouldn't let me.

Extreme Bodies on the Guinness World Records website had somehow managed to record the longest piece of ear hair in the world. It was more than seven inches long, grown by some weird Indian dude halfway across the world. The most pierced woman in the world was a woman in Scotland who had a total of 720 piercings all over her body. One hundred ninety-two of them were on her face alone! I scanned the site on my computer, fascinated and bored at the same time. People were so weird. And so lonely.

Sherman had eaten the banana I left him this morning. He was rapping on the side of his cage, as if trying to get my attention. I went over and checked on him. He'd fallen into his water bowl. Panicked, I scooped him out and shook him a little. Water spilled out of his shell and onto my jeans. Land hermit crabs could die if they were in water too long.

I held the little crab up to my face. His tiny eyes, stuck on the ends of his toothpick-size antennae, stared back at me. "How many times have I told you not to go swimming when I'm not here?" I scolded him. "Huh? How many times?" He snapped at me with a claw. "Oh, I know you don't like to be yelled at. But if you don't listen, then that's what's gonna happen, little man." I let him crawl around on me a little bit until he felt better about things, and then I put him back in his cage. Later I would give him a few crushed Saltines for dinner, maybe even a piece of apple. Sherman had a serious weakness for apples.

Sitting down at my desk, I opened my poetry notebook and wrote down the little paragraph about the house with all the doors shut. It didn't come out as well on paper as it had when I'd said it to Movado the Avocado. But that was the thing about writing. It never did.

Next I opened my journal.

Prompt #5: What is one thing in your life that you wish you could undo?

I swallowed.

Stared at my Snoopy eraser.

Where did Movado the Avocado *get* these questions, anyway?

I stood up.

Paced around the room for a little bit.

Looked out my window. The high school boys were sharing a cigarette on the front porch of the rickety house across the street. They passed it back and forth, holding it between their thumbs and index fingers. I wondered if they ever worried about getting germs. Their basketball sat at the bottom of the steps.

I turned away from the window.

Sat back down at my desk.

Read the prompt again. *What is one thing in your life that you wish you could undo?*

Picked up my pencil.

> The night before Momma left, we got into a huge fight. I don't even remember what started it—just how

it ended. She was in bed again. Actually, she hadn't been out of it for over a week. Dad said her back was acting up, but I knew he was lying. He and Gram both told me to leave her alone and let her sleep, but I didn't want to. Momma's eyes had that weird, zombie look to them, like she was looking right through me when I tried to talk to her. And her skin was so pale that it made the circles under her eyes look almost blue. It freaked me out. "Momma," I kept saying. "Are you okay? Are you sure you feel all right?" I guess I said it too many times, because she went nuts all of a sudden. She started screaming at me. "Leave me alone, May! Just leave me alone!"

She'd done this kind of thing before. And I started to walk out, like I always did. Except that I stopped when I got to her door. For some reason just then, instead of feeling sad, I was just mad. Like, furious mad. I turned around. "What's wrong with you? Why are you even like this?" I said it really, really loud. I guess I might've even screamed it. But I wasn't finished.

I put the pencil down. My fingers, which were cramped from holding it so tightly, were trembling. I could hear my heartbeat thudding in my ears, and my shoulders were up tight around my neck. I needed some air. Walking over to my window, I raised it up high and stuck my head out. Gulped great mouthfuls of hot, humid air. Blech. Still, the pounding in my head had lessened a bit.

I sat back down. Reread what I had just written. I felt like throwing up. I closed the notebook and shoved it inside my book bag. Movado the Avocado could give me all the crap she wanted tomorrow about not finishing my homework. She was just going to have to live with it.

It wasn't going to happen.

Not tonight.

Later in bed, after I had checked my cell phone for probably the eight millionth time, I dialed Olive's number. I didn't hit the send button; I just pressed the receiver to my ear. "I wish I may, I wish I might," I whispered.

I clicked it shut.

After a long, long time, I fell asleep.

32

Tuesday, Wednesday, and Thursday came and went without a single word from Olive. I wasn't exactly getting *used* to my life without her, but I wasn't thinking about it every single second of the day anymore either. Over the next three days, I also finished the primer coat in Movado the Avocado's room and moved on to the paint. Unlike the primer, which was a boring old white color, the paint my teacher had chosen to redo her room with was a pale yellow called Summer Lemon. It wasn't a huge improvement from the white, but at least it was a color. When Movado the Avocado told me that yellow was her favorite color, I laughed.

"What's so funny?" she asked.

"Yellow?" I repeated. "I always thought your favorite

color was green." I pointed to the green V-neck blouse she had on. It had little white polka dots all over it and tied at the throat with a small ribbon. Very tacky. "You *always* wear green."

She touched the side of her hair self-consciously. "They say black is slimming, but I hate black, so that's why I wear so much dark green. It's kind of the next best thing, I guess." She paused. "But I do love yellow."

I didn't say much after that. For the first time, it occurred to me that maybe I wasn't the only one who was aware of Movado the Avocado's shape. Maybe she thought she looked a little off balance too. Maybe it even bothered her a little.

We didn't go anywhere on Tuesday, Wednesday, or Thursday, much to my disappointment. I wouldn't have cared if Movado the Avocado took me back to one of the places we had already been—just as long as we got out of the classroom. But it was not to be. Instead we read "The Raven," a long, horrible poem by Edgar Allan Poe. At first I thought it was some kind of punishment because I hadn't finished my journals, but Movado the Avocado said no, we had to do it anyway. She did, however, expect me to make up the missing journal work. I still hadn't done it. I didn't know if I would.

It took us both days to finish "The Raven," mostly

because it was so long, but also because I complained through the whole thing. If there was a word or two in "Harlem" that I hadn't known, "The Raven" had about fifty. And they were words like "surcease" and "obeisance" and "decorum." I never even knew these words *existed*, much less heard them before. And how was I supposed to remember what they all meant, as we went through the poem and tried to figure out the whole story behind it? I was so glad when it was over that I almost didn't care we hadn't gone out.

Almost.

On Friday, though, as I finished up the wall opposite Movado the Avocado's blackboard, I turned around to find her standing next to her desk. Her purse was on her shoulder. I tried to sound nonchalant. "Are we going somewhere?"

"We are." Movado the Avocado smiled. "I thought we'd try to work on personification somewhere else." Personification was one of the literary terms from "The Raven." All it meant was that an object had been given some kind of human characteristic, like the bird being able to speak in Poe's poem. I didn't care what we were going to work on, just as long as it was away from here.

"Finally!" I hopped down from the ladder, tore off my smock, and put the paint supplies away. "It's about time!"

Movado the Avocado had an amused look on her face. "You enjoy our excursions, then?"

I frowned. "Excursions?"

"When we go out," she said. "Leave the building. Go other places outside of the classroom."

"Oh. Yeah." I shoved my hands in my pockets. "You know. Kinda."

She put her arm around me as we walked out the door. "I'm glad," she said. "I like them too."

33

This time, Movado the Avocado led me to her car, which was parked in the faculty parking lot next to the school. It was a small blue Honda with light brown seats. Shiny, as if it had just been waxed. Not a nick or a scratch in sight.

"We're driving?" I asked.

Movado the Avocado opened her door. "Lucky you." She grinned. "Don't worry. We're not going far."

I got in. The inside of her car smelled like butterscotch and pumpkin. I wondered if she ate butterscotch candies all day long. Maybe she had a stash in the glove compartment. An orange cardboard leaf dangled from the rear-view mirror. Maybe that was where the pumpkin smell was coming from.

Movado the Avocado started the engine. I kept my elbows pressed tightly against my ribs. It was weird sitting so close to her. She reached up and lowered the visor over her head. Underneath, a thick plastic sleeve displayed a neat collection of CDs. She took one out and blew on the back of it. "Do you like Judy Garland?" she asked.

I shook my head. "No."

"Do you know who Judy Garland is?"

"No."

She laughed. "Have you ever heard of the song 'Somewhere Over the Rainbow'?"

I watched as she inserted the CD into the stereo. "You mean from *The Wizard of Oz*?"

"The one and only."

"Well, *yeah*. Everyone's heard of that song."

"Judy Garland sings it." Movado the Avocado put the car in reverse and pulled out of the parking lot. "She was Dorothy in the movie, too."

"Somewhere Over the Rainbow" began to fill the inside of the car. Hearing it reminded me of the time Momma and I had watched *The Wizard of Oz* on TV. I was about six years old. I thought there was something wrong, because the picture on the television was black and white. But when Dorothy opened the door of her house, stepping out into Oz for the first time, and the black and white changed over to color,

I jumped up and down and screamed. It was like magic.

Momma, who had been sitting on the couch with a blanket over her, laughed. "Come over here, you little jumping bean," she said, stretching out her arms. She lifted her blanket and I nestled in close, being careful not to touch her back. Dad brought in a bowl of popcorn right when the flying monkeys grabbed Toto. I fell asleep before the very end, and when I woke up the next morning and asked Momma what had happened, she pushed my hair out of my eyes and said, "Well, she found her way back home, of course."

"How?" I insisted. "How did she find her way back?"

Momma had leaned in close then, her breath tickling my ear. "She clicked her ruby slippers," she whispered. "And they lifted her up and dropped her back in Kansas, just like a dream."

I remembered wanting, *longing* for a pair of ruby slippers after she told me that, just so that I could click them and watch them take me anywhere I wanted.

"May?"

I turned, startled to hear my name.

Movado the Avocado glanced over at me. "I asked you if you'd ever seen *The Wizard of Oz*."

I looked out the window. "No," I said. "Actually, I never got a chance to."

* * *

We drove for another ten minutes or so, leaving downtown Sudbury far behind, and getting on Route 11, which was mostly trees. I could feel my heart slowing down a little as more and more green shaded the side of the road. When Momma and Dad and I used to leave Sudbury for the beach every summer, I had felt this way too, as if we were heading toward a whole other life, full of beauty and light and water. I never wanted to go back to Sudbury. Never.

Now I leaned my head against the window. "Somewhere Over the Rainbow" had been okay, but now Judy Garland was singing some weird song about puppies. Her voice had an odd, throaty sound to it, like she was swallowing marbles while she was singing. I didn't like it. "Where are we going?" I asked finally, as Movado the Avocado made a sudden right turn.

She pulled the car into a roughly formed parking lot and turned off the engine. The squawking Judy Garland came to an abrupt end. "Take a look," she said.

Through the windshield I could make out a small park. Or at least what might have been a small park at one time. Except for a decrepit-looking seesaw, a rusted pair of swings, and a lopsided merry-go-round, it was completely empty. Behind the park, endless rows of cornstalks stretched out like a sea of green; overhead, the sky was a hushed silver color. "Jeez," I said, getting out of the car slowly. "This place looks like a bad movie set. Are you sure Freddy Krueger won't jump out from the corn?"

Movado the Avocado laughed. "It's a park!" She surveyed the small area, her hands on her hips. "Or it was a park." She sighed. "Boy, it does look ancient now, doesn't it?"

"You said it, not me." I followed her as she made her way over to the swings. They were the flexible rubber kind, but the middles were cracked and worn. Movado the Avocado sat in one tentatively, glancing up as the chains squeaked. "So is this another thinking spot?" I asked.

"Not really," she said. "Actually, I haven't been here in years. I just thought it would be a good place to come and practice personification." She swept the entirety of the park with a wave of her hand. "Look at all this stuff we could bring to life!"

I sat down in the swing next to her. "The swings screamed under our weight."

She laughed, leaning back a little and pulling on the swing's chains. "Excellent, May!" I giggled as she swung up higher and higher. The wind swooshed as she swept by, fanning her familiar butterscotch scent into the air. "How about this?" she yelled, looking at me over her shoulder. "The old swing groaned and stretched its rubbery muscles."

I watched her swing back up, her short legs pressed

tightly together, the hems of her brown slacks fluttering around her ankles. "That's a *real* good one," I said, hoping she detected the seriousness in my voice. "You should write that one down."

She flew past me again in a blur of movement. "Lord, I haven't been on a swing in I don't know how long! I forgot how much fun it is!"

Boy, you don't get out much, do you? The rude remark was right on the tip of my tongue. I could taste it. And then in the next second I wondered if it might be true. What if she didn't get out much? She didn't have a husband or kids. It was possible, but I couldn't really see her getting into the whole dating scene. What if the only thing Movado the Avocado had to look forward to on the weekends—besides shopping for green clothes and butterscotch candies—was going to craft fairs with her sister? What if sitting on a swing right now, and feeling that butterfly feeling in the pit of her stomach, really was a big deal? Who was I to criticize that?

I stood up and arranged the seat of the swing along my backside. Then I let myself go, pumping my legs back and forth under me until, in less than a breath, I was flying side by side in the air with Movado the Avocado.

34

We made our way over to the merry-go-round next. I had no idea merry-go-rounds had even been made out of wood before I saw this one. It buckled in the middle, the boards sprained and twisted from the weather, so that when I turned it, hanging on to a teetering handlebar, the whole thing swayed like a ship at sea.

"Get in the middle," Movado the Avocado ordered. "Right in the center there, in between all the handlebars. I'll push."

I sat down obediently and gripped one of the bars. Chips of red paint still clung to the metal like a spattering of blood, and for a moment I felt a little nervous. "Maybe we shouldn't," I said. "I don't think it'll hold."

"Oh, come on!" Movado the Avocado said. She began

to run, hanging on to the bar. Her hair blew back from her face, and she was grinning like a crazy person. I gripped the handlebar more tightly as the dizzy contraption rocked and spun, faster and faster, up and down, until I thought I might fall off completely. "What do you think?" I heard her yell. "Gimme a personification phrase!"

I put my head down as the scenery behind Movado the Avocado blurred into a watercolor. A queasy feeling began to swim around the bottom of my stomach, and my armpits felt hot. "Stop!" I yelled, staring at the rubber siding of my sneaker. This had happened once at the park near Ransom Street, when Olive had twisted my swing all the way up and then stood back, watching me spin crazily back down. I'd puked my guts out after I staggered off, and had to go home."Stop!" I screamed again. I would die if I puked in front of Movado the Avocado. "Please, stop! I feel sick!"

The merry-go-round stopped with a sudden jerk. I lifted my head, blinking to slow the still spinning cornfield behind Movado the Avocado's head.

"Are you okay?" she asked.

I swallowed. "I feel sick."

She reached out her hand. "Come on." I took her hand. It was damp and sweaty. "I'm sorry, May. I got carried away. Come sit down here on the side. Take some deep breaths. You'll be okay."

I let her lead me over to the small wooden edge that lined the outskirts of the park, and sat down, putting my head between my knees. Movado the Avocado made small circles on my back and told me to breathe in. After a few minutes, I felt better. I lifted my head. Drew my hands down the front of my face. "I would've died if I puked in front of you."

"Oh." She dismissed my comment with a wave of her hand. "Don't you think I've had students get sick in front of me before? This past year Jeremy Finkster had the flu and vomited all over the front of my classroom."

"Ugh." I shuddered.

"You can say that again."

"Ugh," I said again.

She laughed. "Actually, vomiting doesn't faze me much. It's blood that makes me a little weak in the stomach. I think it was two years ago when two of my students got into a fistfight, right in the middle of my classroom. One of the boys' noses got broken. There was blood everywhere. I had to go get Mr. Winslow down the hall so I wouldn't faint."

For some reason, this surprised me. I hadn't imagined anything unsettling Movado the Avocado.

She laughed again. "So vomit away, May. As long as I don't see anything red coming out of your mouth, you're good to go with me." I grinned, shoving my hands inside my pockets. I was starting to like the sound of her laugh. It was a nice sound, sort of like a giggle that had been caught in the middle and then turned into a guffaw.

"You know, you really should try again with that book," I said.

"What book?"

"Your book," I answered. "The one you quit on. You should try it again. I mean, you're good at the imagery and personification stuff. Really good. I bet you could do it in a book."

Movado the Avocado looked at me for a minute, as if trying to discern whether or not I was pulling her leg. Then she made a *pppffff* sound with her lips. "I already told you, May. That ship has sailed."

"Why?" I asked. "Why don't you try again? What's the big deal?"

"Well, I don't have the time," Movado the Avocado said. She spread her fingers out in front of her, ticking her reasons off on each one. "I am a full-time English teacher, which means that my work just *begins* after I get home. I have eighty-six students, May. Do you know how much paperwork—how many *essays*—I have to get through? I give three a semester. That makes two hundred fifty-eight essays I have to take home and correct! And that's just for the first semester!"

I shook my head. "Excuses, excuses."

She snorted. "You'll see what I'm talking about when you get older."

"Maybe." I straightened my legs out in front of me. I was disappointed with Movado the Avocado. Her reasons for not trying didn't sound like her. Or at least, they didn't sound like something she'd accept from one of us if we used them on her.

"You know, this place actually isn't so bad," I said. "I mean, now that I don't feel like my guts are gonna come spilling out. I kinda like parks. Me and Olive go to—"

"Olive and I," Movado the Avocado interrupted, correcting me.

"Olive and *I* go to the one over on Charles Street a lot. You know, just to hang out."

I wished I hadn't said that. It made me miss Olive even more.

"That's nice," she said. "I love an empty park. But it really is better when it's just you and a best friend."

I thought about all the times Olive and I had gone down to the Charles Street Park. Just the two of us. It had been more times than I could count. I turned my head. "What did happen with you and Supercali? I mean, that you stopped being friends and everything?"

Movado the Avocado pushed out her bottom lip. It

looked like a big pink caterpillar hanging over her chin. She stared at something in the distance—maybe the seesaw with its peeling orange paint and splintered body—and then sighed heavily. "You want me to tell you the story?" she asked. "What really happened?"

I nodded.

"Okay," she answered. "Well then, I will."

35

"Supercali and I were very different people," Movado the Avocado started. "For one thing, she was an incredible gymnast, just like those girls we saw at the YMCA. But even better. I mean, she was the best gymnast Sudbury High School had ever seen. She actually had a fan club, that's how good she was. Kids would follow her to all her meets just to cheer her on. And when she made it to states in her junior year—and then won—the whole school had a huge assembly to congratulate her."

"Wow," I said softly. "She must've been pretty amazing."

"She was brilliant," Movado the Avocado said.

"Were you a gymnast too?" I asked.

"No." She shook her head slowly. Giggled a little. Softly. "No, I don't think I could turn a cartwheel if you paid me. I was more the quiet type. The bookworm. I was always studying or reading a book or writing a paper. But Supercali and I went way back. We'd been friends since first grade, and so despite the fact that we got into such different things later on, we managed to stay pretty close." She paused. "Until . . ."

I held my breath.

Until what?

Had she kissed Supercali's boyfriend?

Spread a rumor that Supercali had lice?

Maybe she'd gotten jealous of all the attention Supercali received as a gymnast and gone and done something horrible. Something revengelike. The way I had done to her.

"Until the accident," Movado the Avocado said.

"Accident?" I repeated.

"At Emerald Falls," she said. "You've heard of Emerald Falls, right?"

"Of course." Everyone who lived in Sudbury had heard of Emerald Falls. It was a beautiful waterfall set high on Haystack Mountain, a short drive from town. A thick mat of moss grew along the rocks behind the falls, giving the water a slightly greenish tint and consequently its name. Despite its beauty, Emerald Falls was also a dangerous place. Its narrow, slippery ledges and various water depths made it off-limits to everyone under the age of twenty-one. For that reason only, I had never been there. "What were you doing at Emerald Falls?" I asked. "You weren't twenty-one, were you?"

Movado the Avocado shook her head. "We were not. We were just silly, bullheaded sixteen-year-olds who thought nothing could ever hurt us."

"She fell up there?" My voice was soft. "Supercali, I mean? Is that what happened? She fell?"

"We skipped school," Movado the Avocado continued. "Just the two of us. It was a few days after Supercali had won states. Maybe she felt invincible because of her big win, I don't know. Whatever it was, she was dead set on going up to those falls." She sighed, a heavy, wet sound that gurgled inside her throat, and started again. "It hadn't been just the two of us in so long. With her gymnastics and her fan club and everything else going on, we hadn't had a chance to hang out—just us—in what felt like months. I was so happy when she asked me to come. I think if she had asked me to go to the moon with her I would have. Anyway, I guess that was why I didn't put up more of an argument when she suggested the falls. I just said okay. And then we went."

I felt a little nervous listening to Movado the Avocado. I was pretty sure the story involved Supercali getting hurt—which I didn't want to hear about. Somehow, in some way, she'd come to mean a little something to me over these past few weeks with her ice cream sundae toppings, and wanting to see the world. The thought of her getting hurt—on Emerald Falls!—was almost too much to think about. But then the part about why they had stopped being friends would come. And I wanted to hear that part. I needed to hear that part.

"It was the most beautiful day," Movado the Avocado said. "The middle of May, but warm, like July. Hot, even. No clouds. Just a big bowl of blue overhead. I remember it being cooler on the mountain, and then cooler still on the falls, where the water sprayed and misted over us. We lay there on top of the falls for the longest time, staring up at the sky between the leaves of the trees, talking just like we used to do when we were little kids. I think—no, I *know*—that that was the happiest morning of my life." She inhaled sharply, as if bracing herself. "And then Supercali stood up. She said, 'Come on, this is boring. Let's jump.'"

"Into the falls?" I asked.

Movado the Avocado nodded. "Into the falls."

I bit my lip.

"I went first."

"*You* went first?" I repeated. "For real?"

She smiled sadly. "I was a kid once too, May."

"I know." I picked at the toe of my sneaker, embarrassed.

"I was terrified," she continued. "But I did it. I jumped. I remember feeling like I was flying and having a heart attack at the same time. The water was so cold that it took my breath away. But I came back up and waved to Supercali. She screamed and jumped up and down and told me to wait right there, that she was coming." Movado the Avocado closed her eyes. "I told her to do a flip. I knew she could. I'd seen Supercali do two and a half flips with a twist off the balance beam and land perfectly." She pressed her lips together. "So she did."

My shoulders were up around my ears, as if I was right there, watching Supercali. She probably would have balanced her toes along the edge, just like the gymnasts at the YMCA had done, maybe put her arms out to the sides. And then leaped.

"She landed wrong," Movado the Avocado whispered. "She rotated too fast and hit the water like a brick." She drew her hand over her eyes, trying to shield the ugly picture. "I got a bad feeling as soon as she hit the water. Her body made a smacking sound, like a gunshot. To this day, I can still hear it. But then, when she didn't come up . . ." She scanned the gravel in front of us, as if searching for that same spot all over again. "I knew something had happened. Something bad."

"But you got her out."

"I did," Movado the Avocado said. "I got her out and ran for help. Luckily, there was a couple hiking just a little ways off. They ran back and called 911. An ambulance came and got her about ten minutes later."

"She had to go to the hospital?" I asked.

Movado the Avocado nodded. She was very far away now. "For a long time," she answered.

"And then . . . then she healed, right? She was okay and everything? After?"

She nodded again, but it was more like a half nod, as if she didn't quite believe it. "Parts of her healed," she said. "Other parts . . . well . . ." She stopped talking, letting the thought drift off into the sky overhead.

"Well, at least she didn't die," I said. "It could've been a lot worse. You know. If she died, I mean." I paused. "Right?"

Movado the Avocado didn't answer.

I gave her a little nudge. "Right?"

"Absolutely." Her voice was fragile as an egg.

36

The ride back to school was subdued. Movado the Avocado had gotten up after she told me about the accident and headed back to the car. She started the engine and sat there for a moment as Judy Garland filled the car again. She still hadn't told me the most important part of the story, but I wasn't sure if I had the nerve to ask her about it. After everything she'd just told me, I didn't know if I'd ever have the nerve to ask her anything again. It was pretty deep stuff.

A new Judy Garland song began to play. Ugh. The woman's voice was like nails going down a glass wall. I had to drown it out.

"Um . . ." I cleared my throat.

Movado the Avocado leaned over and turned down the volume. "Yes?"

"You don't have to answer this if you don't want. I mean, I know you've just told me a lot of pretty heavy stuff."

"Go ahead." Her voice was gentle.

"Okay, well, so why'd you guys stop being friends after the accident? I mean, was it 'cause you just felt guilty? About telling her to do the flip? Because it really wasn't your fault, you know. I mean, Supercali was the one who started the whole thing to begin with, skipping school, and wanting to go to the falls. I mean, she was even the one whose idea it was to jump off the falls, right?"

Movado the Avocado exhaled forcibly, as if she had been holding her breath while I spoke. She didn't answer right away. In fact, I was just starting to wonder if she had heard my original question. Then she reset her hands on the wheel. "Supercali's parents blamed me," she said, "after they found out the details about what happened. You know, that I had yelled out to her to do the flip. They told my parents that I had encouraged their daughter to act recklessly."

"You?" I asked. "What about Supercali? She's the one who went and did it!"

Movado the Avocado shrugged. "It was both of our faults. But parents are parents. It was hard for them to see Supercali's role in it—especially since she was hurt so badly. I guess it was easier to point the finger at me instead. Anyway, they refused to let me see her while she was in the hospital, and by the time Supercali got home, she had pretty much taken her parents' side. After that, she didn't want anything to do with me anymore."

I looked back out the window. The green was rushing past again. In a few minutes, it would be brown and vacant. "Well, that's totally not fair. Besides, it wasn't even her parents' problem. It was yours and Supercali's."

"Well, no, it *was* her parents' problem," Movado the Avocado corrected me. "They were the ones who almost lost a daughter. They were the ones who had to deal with the aftermath. They had to watch their daughter undergo three surgeries, and then months of rehabilitation."

I shrugged. "Well, did you at least try?"

"Try what?"

"Try to explain things. Your side, I mean. Later. Like in school or whatever? Or did you call her? Anything?"

"Once," she replied. "I called the house when I knew her mother would be out. It was a few weeks after she'd gotten home. Supercali picked up the phone. I couldn't even say anything, I was so nervous. I was just sort of breathing in and out." Movado the Avocado bit her lip. "Supercali said, 'I know this is you, Violet. Don't call me again.' And then she hung up." She shrugged. "And that was that."

"You never tried again?" I asked.

"No." Movado the Avocado's fingers tightened around the wheel. "That was the only time."

The car rolled along soundlessly, except for Judy Garland, who was now warbling horribly about a star in the sky. I wondered if I would have kept trying, if I had been where Movado the Avocado had been all those years ago. If waiting Olive out was an indication, the answer would probably be no. But now, as I thought about it, I honestly wasn't sure. How did you know if you were supposed to keep trying? Was anyone worth that kind of feeling? That embarrassment?

A familiar-sounding tune drifted out of the stereo. I leaned in closer, as if I was imagining it. "Can you turn that up?" I asked. In less than three seconds, strains of "Moon River" began to bleed out of the stereo. The only time I'd ever heard "Moon River" was when Dad or I played it on the harmonica. And Dad had never sung the words. Now I listened, barely even breathing, as Judy Garland's voice filled the car.

She sang about Moon River as if the water was a real person. She and the river were going to drift along together, toward whatever lay ahead, just the two of them. It was a perfect example of personification, I realized suddenly. But it also made me think about about Movado the Avocado and Supercali's friendship, and then Olive's and mine. Olive and I hadn't had plans to go drifting around anywhere together, but it had been just the two of us. For a good long while. Just like it used to be Movado and Supercali. Before everything happened.

I missed Olive so much.

Tears slid down my face before I even realized I was crying.

Movado the Avocado pulled the car off to the side of the road and turned off the stereo. "May." Her voice was soft. "What is it?"

I put my face in my hands and held my breath. But that just made me cry harder. I pressed my fingers into my eyes, wishing for a moment that I could disappear. Maybe the car seat would open up under me and swallow me whole. Anything.

"May." Movado the Avocado's hand was on my shoulder.

I shrugged it off. Breathed in really deeply through my nostrils. Swiped at the tears still rolling down my cheeks. "I'm fine," I said. "Really. I am. Can we just go now?"

Movado the Avocado didn't move.

"Seriously." I glared at her. "I just want to go. Please."

"All right." She steered the car back onto the road. Drove for a few minutes without saying anything. I kept my face pointed toward the window.

"May," she said finally, as we made our way back through downtown Sudbury. "I just want you to know that—"

"Don't, okay?" I cut her off. I knew she was going to say something really corny, like "You don't have to be ashamed to express your feelings to me," or "Don't ever be afraid to cry." Something totally fake and bogus like the guidance counselor had told me a million times this year. All crap. Teachers and guidance counselors and adults in general didn't know anything about real feelings or what they did to you. They had no friggin' *idea*.

Movado the Avocado's mouth opened and then shut again, like a fish. She pulled her car into the faculty parking lot and put it into park.

I stared out the window. "We're done, right? I don't have to go back inside again, do I?"

"No." I tried to ignore the fact that Movado the Avocado's voice sounded sad. She was a big girl. She'd get over it.

"Okay," I said, pushing open the car door. "See you Monday, then."

37

It had been six days, but Olive still hadn't texted me. She hadn't sent me anything on my MySpace page either. True, I wasn't thinking about it 24-7 anymore, but when I did, it still hurt.

It had just been a matter of time, really. First it was Brittany and her crowd. Now it was Olive's turn, I guess. She'd stuck it out as long as she could. People could only be pushed so far. Dad had said that to me once, when he was trying to explain things about Momma. *She could only be pushed so far, May. It's the same with everyone. People can only take so much.* That was where Olive was now, I guessed. She'd been pushed too far. She could only take so much.

"I'm going out for a while," I said, ducking my head

inside Gram's room. It was Friday evening, still light out. Dad wouldn't be home for at least another hour.

"Where will you be?" Gram was playing her millionth game of solitaire.

I didn't know. Anywhere but here. A nagging mosquito thing was flitting around in the back of my head. It was just out of reach, but buzzing in and around with a vengeance. Maybe some fresh air would shut it up.

"Just for a walk," I said. "I won't be long."

If there's anything I hate more than being seen wandering around the neighborhood alone, I don't know what it is. *I'm* okay with being alone, but I don't want people to see me that way, as if I'm advertising the fact that I don't have any friends. One time when I ran over to the Charles Street Park to meet Olive, she was the only one there. She was sitting on one of the black rubber swings, just swinging slowly, her feet dragging a little in the dust. It made me want to cry, seeing her like that. Alone, I mean. It felt as if something was tugging inside my chest. I hurried over and sat down next to her.

Now I kept what I hoped was a hurried, distracted look on my face as I went up and down the streets, like I was late getting somewhere I had to be. It was almost six o'clock, but it was really hot. Like, unbearably hot. The air against my face felt as if someone had just taken a T-shirt out of the dryer and smushed it over my nose and mouth. The smell of fried chicken and old cigarettes was everywhere. It made me thirsty.

I tried to concentrate on the buzzing mosquito thing inside my head, but I was too uncomfortable. Heading toward the shadier part of the neighborhood, I found myself at the corner of Olive's street. Her house was all the way down at the opposite end. I walked down the length of sidewalk slowly, ready to dart behind a car or into a driveway if I saw her. But Vine Street was a quiet street. There were only a couple of cars parked along the curb. Everyone's windows were shut tight, probably because they had the air conditioner on. Not many people on Ransom Street had air conditioners. The lawns were neat and green, with clipped bushes and small rows of flowers leading up to the front porches.

I crossed the street when I reached Olive's house and hid behind a tree. The house was a two-story brick with a white door and shutters. Clusters of blue hollyhock shrubs sat under the front bay window, and a flag with a picture of two white cats was hung out in front. Olive's mother loved cats. Their mailbox, which was on the front of the house next to the door, was in the shape of a cat head. It even had little iron ears sticking out of the top.

I wondered if Olive was inside. If she was in her room,

listening to one of her Beatles CDs. Maybe she was lying on her bed, staring up at the poster of John Lennon, wondering what it would feel like to have his arms around her. Olive had never been kissed. She'd told me that once, last year, after Paul Samuelson had practically sucked my face off during the spring dance. She'd asked me later what it had felt like. I told her she wasn't missing much.

The front door of her house opened. I turned sideways behind the tree, sucking in my stomach, hardly daring to breathe. Across the street, I could hear Olive and her mother walking down the front steps.

"I don't understand why you took so long to ask me," Mrs. Masters said. "It just seems so silly, honey. They're just *shoes*, for heaven's sake. Why would you think I would say no?"

"I don't know." Olive paused. "They're just so different from anything I wear. Really different. For me, I mean."

"Well, you might laugh when I tell you this, but I wore Doc Martens when I was your age too." I could hear the *click-click* of Olive's mother's heels against the sidewalk, and then the sound of the car door being opened.

"You did?" Olive sounded shocked and pleased at the same time. "Seriously?"

The conversation faded as Olive shut her own door and her mother started up the car. I leaned even farther into the tree, as if I could somehow meld myself into the wood, until the car backed out of the driveway toward me. It shot forward in the opposite direction, leaving me there, still huddled behind the tree.

After a while, I turned around and went home.

There was nowhere else to go.

38

"May!"

I cringed as Dad shouted my name from the living room. It was Saturday afternoon. He was back on the couch, feet up on the coffee table, watching a *Jaws* marathon. I'd already seen all the *Jaws* movies. They were boring. The shark looked totally fake. You could actually *see* the wires inside its mouth if you looked closely enough. I didn't feel like watching any of them again. "What?"

"Come out here for a minute! I want to talk to you!"

I got up from my computer, where I'd been staring at a picture of the largest swimming pool in the world. It was in Chile, and it was nineteen acres long. That was the size of at least three football fields. Who *were* these people?

"About what?" I asked, standing in my doorway.

Dad patted the couch next to him. "Over here. Have a seat."

"I'm on the computer."

Dad tilted his chin toward his chest, and looked at me.

"All right, all right." I walked over to the couch and plopped down. "What?"

"How've you been?"

"Fine."

"How's Olive?"

"Fine."

"You get any time in at the pool yet?"

"Nope."

Dad looked at me. I stared at the TV. It was the first *Jaws*. Out of all of them, I liked it the most. The mechanical shark was ripping some dude's stomach out. It was pretty gory.

"How about summer school?" Dad asked. "How's that going?"

"We already talked about that!"

"Well, I want to know more," Dad said. He reached over and grabbed a handful of Doritos out of a bowl.

"I already told you. It's *okay*."

"What's 'okay' mean, May? What're you doing? Specifically?"

I sighed. Heavily. "It's just me and Miss Movado. She's

teaching me poetry again and making me keep a journal."

Dad sat up a little. "What do you mean, just you and Miss Movado? Where are the other kids?"

"I don't know," I answered truthfully. "She said it was just the two of us."

Dad's eyebrows narrowed. "That's strange. I've never heard of a teacher having one student for summer school." He paused and then shoved a few more chips into his mouth. "So what's she having you do? Poetry and writing?"

I nodded, grabbing a few chips from the bowl. "*And* she's making me paint her whole room over."

"Well, good," Dad said. "I didn't know about the whole one-on-one deal, but I'm glad they listened to something I said."

"Listened to you?" I asked. "What do you mean?"

"That was my idea," he said. "Having you repaint her room, I mean. I suggested it to Principal Mola."

I stopped chewing. "*You* suggested it? When?"

"On the phone before that whole meeting you had with him," Dad said. "I couldn't come down to the school, but Mola explained everything to me, told me what you'd done, and asked if I had any suggestions." He shrugged. "So that's what I suggested."

I sat up all the way until my back was ramrod straight against the couch. "*You're* the one who's responsible for me having to tape and prime and paint an entire classroom?" I asked. "For the whole summer? Are you *kidding* me?"

"Don't shout," Dad said.

I stood up. "I can't believe this!" I stamped my foot. "I cannot believe this! My own father, selling me out to some psycho English teacher, just so that—"

Dad rose up from the couch like a tree. "Selling you out?" he repeated. "Selling you *out*? I saved your butt, May; I didn't sell you out! Mola was hell-bent on having you expelled! If I hadn't come up with that idea—*any* idea—you'd be having this conversation with me in an entirely different school!"

His eyes were flashing, and he was doing that finger-point in my face again.

"I wish it was you that was gone!" I screamed. "Not Momma! I wish it was you!"

He stared at me for a few seconds. Then he lowered his arm, wiping a drop of spit at the corner of his mouth with the back of his wrist. "You don't mean that." His voice was soft.

"I do mean it!" I screamed, despite the fact that the look on his face as I said it almost broke me in two. "I *do* mean it! I wish it was *you* that was gone—you, you, *you*!"

A muscle in Dad's jaw tightened. He looked down at the floor. Brushed chip crumbs off the front of his jeans.

"Someday," he said finally, raising his head and putting his hands on his hips, "you'll regret saying that, May. Maybe not now, maybe not soon, but someday you will regret it. I promise you."

And with that, he put on his boots and walked out of the house.

39

I stood stock-still after Dad walked out. It was like my feet were frozen to the floor. Dad had never walked out in the middle of the day, or after one of our arguments. Never. He was more of a yeller and thrower like me.

A few weeks after Momma left, he had destroyed the kitchen, hurling pots and pans and the pasta colander, even Gram's heavy cast-iron skillet, which she used to make the bangers and mash, into the living room with such force that I thought they were going to go through the walls. Mr. Reynolds had a conniption with the broom handle that night, sending Dad into even more of a rage. Gram and I stayed in her room, listening to the two of them scream it out downstairs. Afterward, though, Dad had come back up. He looked worn out. His hands were trembling. He picked up all the pots and pans and, without a single word, put them back inside the cupboard. He pulled out the pillow from the hall closet and put it on the couch and lay down. And then he fell asleep.

I didn't know what his leaving now meant. And not knowing, for some reason, was even scarier than knowing. I bolted out the door after him.

But it was too late. He was nowhere in sight.

Worse, his truck was missing from its usual place on the street.

If my feet had been frozen before, now they were on fire. I ran blindly up and down streets, jumping over curbs and gutters, swerving around fire hydrants and trash bags and dog poop and dirty soda cups. I ran and ran and ran, with no destination, just to run, to get away, to leave it all behind. When it became physically impossible to take a breath without a searing pain cutting into my lungs, I stopped. Tried to breathe normally again. The effort it required—just to inhale—made tears come to my eyes. I wiped them away furiously. But the action made me cry even harder. And before I knew it, I was sitting on the edge of a curb of a street I had never been on before, crying like a little baby. This was nothing like what I had done in Movado the Avocado's car. That had been a little wellspring of emotion, a wetting of the eyes. This was a torrent. A monsoon. I put my head down so no one would see me. And then I cried harder.

I cried for so long and so violently that for a moment, in between my sobs, I was afraid a leak had sprung somewhere inside of me. It felt as if my insides were emptying out—stomach, brain, heart, all of it, a big sloppy mess, just spilling out of my mouth and nose and eyes.

Eventually, though, it ended. My nose was packed full of dribbly snot and my eyes were swollen, but it ended. I wiped my face on the bottom of my shirt, and blew my nose into a corner of it, where no one would see. The sun was low behind the trees, and the sky was a dusky blue, dotted with a few flimsy clouds. It was probably close to five o'clock. Gram would be wondering where I was. But I didn't move. I couldn't. I felt like an overcooked noodle—as if I'd spent the last drop of my entire energy reserve. I put my head back down. I'd wait a few minutes until it refilled. And then I'd figure out what to do next.

All of a sudden, as if the mosquito inside my head had suddenly gotten tired and landed, I realized what it was that had been nagging at me these past two days. Perfectly clearly, too, as if someone had put a whole other pair of eyes into my sockets, or turned my head around in the opposite direction.

I know this is you, Violet. Don't call me again.

I was glad I was sitting.

If I had been standing up, I might have fallen down.

I glanced wildly around the street. Someone had thrown a handful of ketchup packets along the curb; there was an empty bottle of Mountain Dew, a tattered green mitten. Farther down, there was a bunched-up diaper, the taped ends clotted with dirt and gravel. I looked away in disgust.

I hated it here.

I hated everything.

And everybody.

It didn't matter how hard you tried or what you did—life still came at you from every possible angle, trying to knock you down.

Again.

And again.

And again.

40

I darted into the Rite Aid at the corner, slowing as the electric doors yawned wide to let me in. The hair on my arms prickled as the air-conditioning enveloped my hot skin. An elderly woman standing at the end of a long line in front of the checkout nodded hello. She was reading a *Good Housekeeping* magazine and eating a bag of M&M's. In front of her were at least six other people waiting to pay for their items. The cashier behind the counter was punching keys and shoving items into plastic bags. She looked irritated.

I began to pace up and down the aisles, staring stupidly at boxes of hair color and eye shadow. The next aisle contained facial creams and acne treatments. I grabbed a red and white box of some kind of face cream. The price tag said $49.99. I shoved it inside the waistband of my jeans and let my shirt hang loosely over it. Put my head down and kept going. Aisle 3B was stocked with school supplies. Paper, pens, magic markers, notebooks. I skimmed the wall for a moment, settling on a bright red lock that I could use next year for my locker. $10.99. I shoved it inside the waistband at the back of my pants. Put my head down. Kept going.

In the span of seven minutes, I had inserted four other items into the front and back pockets of my jeans:

a bag of honey-roasted peanuts ($1.19)
a toothbrush (3.29)
a package of hair elastic (4.99)
a bottle of purple nail polish (4.89)

I didn't eat peanuts. I'd never used nail polish in my entire life. I had more toothbrushes at home than I would ever need. And I had a supersize bottle of Momma's old face cream in our bathroom medicine cabinet that would probably last me until Christmas. It didn't matter. Nothing mattered anymore.

The elderly woman, who was still reading her *Good Housekeeping* magazine, had gotten significantly closer to the front of the line. In front of her, a young woman was arguing about the price of a bottle of shampoo with the cashier, who, if she had looked irritated before, now looked as if she wanted to rip someone's head off with her bare hands.

I put my head down, walked out the electric doors into the stifling heat, and headed home.

41

Gram was sitting on the edge of the couch in the living room when I walked in. Her hands were flat against her knees, and she was staring at the TV, which was off. Except for the occasional visit to the kitchen, I hadn't seen Gram anywhere in the past year except her room. "Gram?" I asked. "Are you all right?"

She didn't move. I took a few steps closer. "Gram?"

"Where did your father go?" she asked.

"I don't know." I picked at my thumbnail. "We had a fight and—"

"I know you had a fight." Gram's voice was brusque. "I heard you. Like always."

The only time I'd ever heard her use this tone of voice was with Dad, the night before Momma left. She'd been defending me, ordering him to back off and leave me alone. I was entitled to my feelings, she'd said, whatever they were.

Now I began to work the inside of my cheek with my teeth, while at the same time patting my waist carefully to make sure my contraband had not slipped. "Did you eat—"

"I heard what you said to him, May." She cut me off abruptly with that same brusqueness, and then turned around and looked at me. "How could you? How could you say something like that to your own father?"

I looked down at my shoes. Felt the edge of the face cream package dig into the soft part of my belly. Looked back up. "You should talk," I said.

Gram drew back. She looked shocked, almost frightened. I'd never once, in all my thirteen years, said anything rude to her. I hadn't even come close. Right now, though, it didn't matter. I felt like a runaway train, going a hundred miles an hour with no sign of stopping or even slowing down. People needed to stand back—far, far back—before they got hurt.

"I've never said anything like that to your father," Gram said.

"Not with words," I heard myself saying. "But you've said the same thing I did, Gram, by not saying anything at all. You lie there in your room all day like Momma left only you and not us, too. It's like you don't care whether we're around or not."

Gram stood up. She swayed a little in her pink bootie slippers and steadied herself on the edge of the couch. Her hair was still matted above her ear, and that stupid housecoat collar was still folded under. "You have no right to say that to me." The sternness in her voice was gone; now it sounded broken. "You can't know what it's like to have your only child leave you, May."

I lifted my chin.

Bit down hard on my tongue so that the tears wouldn't come.

"But I know what it's like to have your only mother leave," I said.

We stood there for a few moments, Gram and me, regarding each other. I didn't know what it was she saw as she looked at me, but for the first time in my life, I saw a stranger as I looked at her. Even with her going to bed and playing solitaire and pretty much being a recluse these last eighteen months, there had still been a part of the Gram that I knew somewhere in there. I couldn't see it now. Now it felt as if I was looking at someone I had never known.

"It's not the same," Gram whispered. She shook her head as if to convince herself of this fact, and smoothed down the front of her housecoat. "It's not the same thing at all."

I stood there for a moment as she shuffled back into her room and shut the door. And as I stared at the opaque TV screen, I realized that I was completely alone.

The fact took my breath away.

My knees gave out, and I sank to the floor, steadying myself against it with the palms of my hands. The red lock fell out of my waistband; two seconds later, so did the face cream. I didn't look at them. My brain felt as if it was spinning on its own orbit; my breaths came in short gasps. This was even worse than how it had felt after Momma left. Part of me back then, I realized, must have understood that I still had Gram and Dad. And Olive, too. Now they were all gone too—or at least on completely different planes.

It was just me now.

Me, and no one else.

42

I staggered back into my room and closed the door. After a few minutes, I yanked everything out of my pants—peanuts, red lock, toothbrush, hair ties—and threw them on my bed along with the face cream and the purple nail polish. I stared at the pile for a moment. It was all there, right in front of me. Actual, hardened proof that I was in fact a no-good nothing. Of course, I'd already known this. Maybe Principal Mola had known too. And Movado the Avocado. I sat down at my desk. Tore open my journal notebook. Flipped to the page about my last night with Momma. Staring at the words in front me, I felt an unbearable pain inside, a whirlpool kind of pain that sucked me down and spun me around, thrusting me deeper and deeper into a black void. There was no going back. It was now or never.

I reread the few lines of the last paragraph I had written:

> *For some reason just then, instead of feeling sad, I was just mad. Like, furious mad. I turned around. "What's wrong with you? Why are you even like this?" I said it really, really loud. I guess I might've even screamed it. But I wasn't finished.*

I picked up my pencil.

Gritted my teeth.

Leaned in and began to write.

> *Momma just looked at me when I yelled at her, like she didn't understand why I was asking her why she was the way she was. And that made me even madder. "You're a terrible mom!" I yelled. "All you do is lay here in bed and feel sorry for yourself all the time! You don't do anything! I hate your guts! I wish I had someone else for a mother!"*

I stopped writing. Actually, I had to stop writing, because I was squeezing the pencil so hard that it snapped in half. I sat there for a minute, just staring at the jagged yellow wood.

I hadn't meant any of it. I swear to God I hadn't. I just hadn't known how to tell her what I was really thinking. That I missed her. That I was so lonely without her that it felt as if part of me was actually disappearing. That every time she walked into her room and closed the door, she shut me out. Sometimes for days at a time. And that when she did that, I felt like a nobody. As if I didn't matter. I didn't have words for all of that. And so the other side of it had come out. The angry side. The mean side. The bad side.

Dad had come in that night when he heard me yelling at Momma. He'd smacked me—right across the face. I'm still not mad at him for doing that. If he hadn't, I don't know what other terrible things I would have said. But it hurt. My cheek stung and my eyes filled up with tears. I ran out of Momma's room and into mine.

Behind my door, I could hear Gram chastising Dad. She was using that voice of hers, telling him that he had no right to lay a hand on me. He told her to stay out of it, that I was his daughter and he would lay a hand on me when he saw fit. And that after the things I had just said to Momma, he had seen fit. It went on for a few more minutes after that, neither of them backing down.

Then there was the sound of a door slamming.

And then another.

It was the last time any of us talked to Momma again.

43

For some reason, my eyes drifted over to the next page of my journal.

Prompt #8, it read. *What are three things you know for sure?*

I picked up my jagged pencil again.

1. I know that Momma left because of the things I said to her.

2. I know that she is never coming back.

3. I know that I don't care.

I stared at number three for a long time.

Then I picked up the other half of the pencil and erased it.

I stared at the faint pencil marks left behind on the page.

I picked up my pencil again and retraced them, very lightly.

I know that I don't care.

And then I erased it once more.

For good this time.

I lay on my bed for a long, long time until I finally reached for my cell phone. I flipped it open, staring at the only number still left in my contacts. I clicked it shut again. Olive was probably out with her parents, wearing her new shoes. And even if she picked up after seeing it was me, she probably wouldn't be able to talk—if she *did* want to talk—in front of her mom.

I rolled over on my bed. My ribs dug into the plastic edge of the toothbrush case. I picked it up. Stared at it for a long time. Then I sat back up. Flicked open my phone again. Dialed Olive's number. My fingers were shaking.

She picked up on the third ring. "Hello?"

For about three seconds, I couldn't speak. Literally. It was like my voice had gotten stuck in between my throat and my mouth.

"Hello?" Olive asked again. "May? Is that you?"

"Yeah," I said finally. I got up from my bed and started

walking around my room. It felt like my heart might explode otherwise. "Listen. I want to apologize for all the things I said to you. I just got so mad and I didn't think and . . ." I sounded so stupid. I wasn't any good at this. I wasn't making any sense.

"Thanks," Olive said. "I want to apologize too. I should never have said anything about you feeling sorry for yourself. I don't know what it's been like for you, May. Not really. And I shouldn't have been so mean about it."

I nodded, as if Olive could hear me on the other end of the phone. She was definitely the best friend I'd ever had. Maybe the best friend I'd ever have.

"May?" Olive asked. "Are you okay?"

Was I okay? Of course I was okay. I'd been okay since the last worst day of my entire life. I'd been okay over the past eighteen months, getting up every morning like a robot, putting one foot in front of the other to make it through the day, and when that finally got too hard, letting all the other parts inside of me—the ones that were trying so hard to sit still and be quiet—yell and blow up. "No," I whispered. "I'm not okay."

"What's wrong?"

"I was just . . . wondering if maybe . . ." I shook my head. Why had it taken me so long to apologize? And why was telling her that I needed her now so hard? *Why?* Why hadn't I been able to say it to Momma? Why hadn't any of us?

"Maybe what?" Olive pressed.

I swallowed. Grabbed the skin at the front of my throat and pulled, as if willing the words to come out.

"May?" Olive asked. "Do you need me to come over?"

"Yeah." I nodded quickly, up and down, up and down. "I do."

"Gimme ten minutes," she said. "I'll be right there."

44

I sat down at the top of the steps, waiting for Olive. When I saw her open our door, I gave a little yell, almost as if I hadn't quite believed she would really come. "Hi," I said, checking my enthusiasm a little as I let her in. She gave me a hug. Her hair smelled faintly of sunflower seeds. I hugged her back. The tugging feeling inside my chest eased a little.

She glanced up the stairs anxiously. "Is your dad home?"

I shook my head. "No, he went out." I pushed down the annoyance I felt as Olive's face registered relief. I couldn't blame her, really, for being a little scared of Dad. She wasn't used to all the yelling and carrying on. And maybe that was a good thing.

I glanced down at her feet as we climbed the steps. "Nice shoes," I said casually. "When did you get them?"

Olive paused on the step and hitched up her jeans. Her bright blue Doc Martens went all the way up to her calf. "Yesterday," she said. "Do you like them?"

"Yeah," I said. "They look great on you."

"I think they do too." Olive tilted one shoe to the left and then to the right, admiring the blue leather under the dim light. "I love them."

We went into my room. Olive had been in my room only a handful of times, but she always did the same thing when she came over. I watched now as she headed directly for Sherman and lifted him out of his cage. "How's Sherman?" she cooed, letting the little crab stare at her for a moment. Sherman shrank into his shell a little, and then scuttled backward on Olive's arm.

"He's confused," I said. "He hasn't seen you in so long."

"Ohhhh." Olive sounded disappointed. "Shermie-Sherm. It's me! It's Olive. You remember me, don'tcha?"

I sat down on the other side of my bed. "Olive."

She was wiggling her fingers, still trying to coax Sherman out of his shell.

"Olive." I said it louder this time.

She didn't look over. "Yeah?"

"I did something."

"Like what?" Olive leaned her head in more closely to the crab. She blew on his face, and then touched his still vanishing head with the tip of her finger.

I stayed quiet.

Now she looked over. "Like what?" she said again. Sherman, apparently relieved that Olive had stopped blowing on him, had finally started to crawl up her arm.

I pointed to the top of my bed. "I stole stuff. This stuff. All of it. From Rite Aid."

Olive glanced down at the items, her eyes roving over them frantically. "Why? Did you need it? I could've gotten you—"

"No." I covered my face with both hands. "I didn't need any of it. I just . . . I don't know. I don't know how to explain it. I just kind of went off."

"What happened?" she asked. Sherman was still making his way up her arm. "Did you have another fight with your dad?"

I nodded. "That . . . and . . ." It all felt so big right now. There was no way I could explain it. "Other stuff," I finished lamely. "I don't know. It was so stupid."

"May." Olive sat down on the bed next to me and draped an arm over my shoulders. "I don't mean to sound awful when I say this, but . . . you're really kind of screwing up your life."

I squeezed my eyes tight. I knew she was right, but that didn't make it any easier to hear.

"You gotta stop it, May. You do. Otherwise, things are gonna get too big for you to fix. You're gonna end up somewhere else, and . . . well, I'm almost a hundred percent sure you and me will probably stop being friends."

I started picking at my thumbnail.

"I don't want to stop being your friend, May," Olive said. "You're the best friend I've ever had."

I snorted.

"No." Olive waited until I looked up at her. Her small eyes had gotten very round. "You are, May. You're the only person in school who's even given me the time of day. I'm pretty sure everybody else thinks I'm invisible. Even when we hung out with Brittany and the rest of those girls, they never talked to me. Not once. They just talked to you."

I tried to think back to when it had been the larger group of us, but it felt too long ago now. How hadn't I noticed that none of them had talked to Olive, though? Had I really been the only one?

"They just let me stay in the group because of you," Olive said. "None of them really wanted me there." She grinned a little. "I can't even tell you how excited I was when you and Brittany finally had that big blowout."

"You're the only friend I have left, Olive." It came out as a whisper. A wobbly whisper. I covered my face again because I was so embarrassed.

"Well, you're the only friend I have, *period*," Olive said. She squeezed my shoulders tight. "And I really want to keep it that way."

My shoulders slumped forward. I was out of answers.

"You have to return these things," Olive said.

I lifted my head again. "Return them? I can't! They'll freak! They'll call the police!"

"Maybe they will," she said. "Maybe they won't. Either way, you have to take this stuff back. It's not yours."

"Well, why don't I just go down and march myself right into the juvenile detention center?" I could feel myself getting panicky. "Because you know that's what's gonna end up happening."

"You're projecting," Olive said calmly.

"I'm *what*?"

"Projecting," she repeated. "Like, you're already deciding what's going to happen before you even do anything. Projecting isn't good. It can freeze you up so that you don't do anything at all."

"Listen, Olive. I appreciate you being here and all, but I can't deal with the life-coach stuff right now, okay? Seriously."

Olive held up her hands. "Okay, okay, fine."

I ran my hands through my hair. Looked frantically around the room, as if the answer might be lying somewhere underneath my dirty clothes heaps.

"That was actually really good," Olive said softly.

"What was?"

"The way you just talked to me." Olive nodded. "You didn't yell or get mean or anything. You just told me you didn't want me to do the life-coach stuff."

I paused. Looked around the room again. Glanced back at Olive. "I did, didn't I?"

She nodded. Held out her hand. "Come on," she said. "I'll go with you to Rite Aid."

45

Olive put all the stolen items into a paper bag and rolled the top down into a makeshift handle. "You carry them," she said. "I'll be right next to you." By the time we left the apartment, it was almost dusk. The air was still heavy with heat, and the sky above was a colorless void. I wondered if the weather was making me feel sick to my stomach, or if it was the thought of what I was about to do.

Still, another, smaller part of me felt a little bit okay with it. Like maybe for the first time, I was doing the right thing. Trying to fix a wrong I had committed. Being accountable for my actions. On my own. I wanted to stop messing up my life, the way Olive had said. I wanted to stop doing dumb, rash things because I was so angry.

I wanted to stop being so angry.

The cashier I had seen on my way in was still there, standing behind the counter. She was a middle-aged woman with light, short hair and a double chin. Except for her and an elderly man pondering a selection of laxatives in Aisle 3, the rest of the store seemed to be empty.

"Come on," Olive whispered, poking me in the back. "No one's here. It's a perfect time. Let's just get this over with."

I walked on leaden legs toward the wide blue counter. The cashier looked up. A name tag pinned to the front of her red smock said DOLORES. Next to it was another pin made out of some kind of yarn. It was a yellow smiley face with plastic, wobbly eyes. I hoped that smiley face was an indication of how nice a person she was. And how forgiving.

"Can I help you?" she asked.

I set the brown paper bag on the counter. Shoved my hands quickly inside my pockets. Stepped on my toe. Hard.

"Do you need to return something?" Dolores asked.

I nodded.

"All right." She reached for the bag. "Do you have a receipt?"

I snatched the bag away from her. Dolores looked startled. "It's—um—I mean—I have to return these things."

"Okay." Dolores glanced over at Olive, as if she might do something alarming too. "You already said that."

"I, um . . . took them." I swallowed hard. "Without paying, I mean. This afternoon. I took them and I left the store. But I know it was wrong, and I'm here to return them and tell you how sorry I am and that it will never happen again." The words came out in a torrent. I did not look up.

"Wait, you *stole* these things?" Dolores snatched the bag away from me again. She yanked it open and began taking the items out. One by one, she laid them out on the counter in front of her. Face cream. Toothbrush. Lock. Hair ties. Nail polish. Peanuts. She put a hand on her hip and cocked her head. "I'm going to have to call the police," she said. "You know that, don't you? It's protocol."

"You don't *have* to call the police," Olive said, stepping forward. "I mean, she just returned everything she took. And she's here now, telling you that she'll never do it again."

Dolores gave Olive a pitiful sort of look that said, *What's a nice girl like you doing hanging out with someone like this?* "How do *I* know she's returned everything?" she said. "She could still have fifty more dollars' worth of stuff at her house." She glared at me. Breathed through her nose like a dragon. "That's the thing about people who steal," she said. "You can't tell when they're telling the truth, either."

"I'm *not* lying," I said, gritting my teeth hard so that I wouldn't yell. "I swear I'm not."

Dolores stared at me a moment. Then she looked back down at the items and pursed her lips. I held my breath. "What's your name?"

"May . . . I mean, Maeve. Maeve O'Toole."

She paused. "Where do you go to school?"

I squinted, as if I hadn't heard her correctly. What did where I went to school have to do with anything?

"You *do* go to school," Dolores asked, "don't you?"

I bit the inside of my cheek. "Sudbury West."

"What grade are you in?"

"I just finished eighth," I said. "I'll be going into ninth."

Dolores made a little clucking sound with her tongue. "Eighth grade," she muttered. "Unbelievable."

I could feel blood roaring in my ears. That was why she asked me these questions? So she could rub it in? Make me feel even worse than I already did?

I watched as she walked around to the front of the counter and held me around the elbow. I yanked it back.

"You have to come in *here*," she said, pointing to a small door off to the side of the store marked EMPLOYEES ONLY. "And I wouldn't start anything if I were you, young lady. You're already in enough trouble as it is."

"Come on." Olive gripped my hand. "Let's just go, May."

46

The room behind the EMPLOYEES ONLY door was very small. In fact, the dusty soda machine pressed against the far wall took up most of the space. It hardly seemed worth it, since the Sprite, 7Up, Coke, Diet Coke, and A&W root beer tabs were all marked OUT OF ORDER. Aside from the defunct soda machine, there was a round table in the middle of the room and two plastic chairs. There was a phone on the wall with at least twenty buttons going up and down the right-hand side. Next to the phone was a work schedule. Various names were listed after the days of the week. Dolores's name was second on the list.

"Sit," Dolores said, pointing to the two chairs. "And don't *touch* anything. I have to ring this guy up, and then I'll be right back."

I put my head down on the table as she closed the door and walked out.

Olive reached out and rubbed my arm. "It'll be okay, May."

I raised my head. "How will it be okay? She's gonna call the police, Olive. They're going to make a record of what I did, take me out—" I stopped suddenly, thinking ahead. "God, do you think they'll put handcuffs on me?"

Olive's forehead creased. "*No.* Jeez, May, you didn't go rob someone at gunpoint. You stole some nail polish. And stuff. They're not going—"

"You know what?" I stood up, shoved my chair under the table. "I don't even care. I don't. They can do whatever they want. They can tie me up, put me in handcuffs, throw me in jail. I don't care."

"Why do you always say that?" Olive asked. She stood up too. Her hands were gripping the back of her chair. "Why do you always say you don't care about anything?"

"Because I don't." I started to pace around the room, which wasn't really like pacing at all because the room was so small, but I had to move. Being inside that room was, like, suffocating. "I don't care. About any of it."

"But you *do* care," said Olive. "You care about a lot of things that you say you don't."

"Like what?"

"Like . . . this situation. You *care* whether or not the police are going to come. You care whether—"

"I don't!" I insisted. "Seriously. I'm done, Olive. I am. I tried to do the right thing, like you suggested, and now it's going to blow up in my face. Just like I tried to get Momma to—" I caught myself before the rest of the sentence came out. Where had that even *come* from, anyway?

"Just like you tried to get your momma to what, May?" Olive's voice was so soft that for a moment, as I inhaled, I felt shaky.

"Nothing." I brushed her off.

"Please," she said. "Tell me, May. What'd you try to get your mother to do?"

"To pay attention to me!" I screamed. "Okay? To stop going into her room every night and shutting the door and locking me out like I didn't exist! Only I didn't know how to say it the right way! I got all mad instead, and it came out all wrong and it was all my fault, Olive! It is all my fault she's gone!"

I was holding on to the chair so hard that when I said the last sentence it buckled underneath my grip. I went down with it, hitting my chin on the edge of the table. The pain was sharp and sudden, like a slap, and before I knew it, my mouth had filled with blood.

"May!" Olive cried, rushing toward me. "Your mouth! You're bleeding!"

"I'm okay," I mumbled, cupping my chin with my hand. "I just cut it a little. My tongue, too, I think." Blood was running over my lips and down my chin in a thin red stream. It tasted salty and unnervingly warm.

"I'll get tissues," Olive said, yanking open the door.

Dolores was standing there. "What's going on?" she asked. "What happened?"

I stood up slowly as another person behind Dolores looked into the room.

"Miss Movado!" Olive said, taking a step back into the room. "We need tissues! May cut her chin!"

Movado the Avocado dug into her purse and extracted a small package of pale yellow tissues.

"What're you doing here?" I asked as she knelt down next to me and pressed a stack of them against my chin.

"Never mind right now," Movado the Avocado said. "Let's get you cleaned up."

47

Dolores showed Movado the Avocado and me through another door marked EMPLOYEES ONLY. This one had a sink and a toilet in it. Above the sink was a dirty soap dispenser, filled with bright pink liquid soap. Pieces of toilet paper littered the floor, and a smell like old Lysol hung in the air.

I let Movado the Avocado do her thing with my chin. She mopped up the blood with the rest of the tissues, and then held a large wad of damp paper towel against it. Turned out there were two cuts—one underneath my chin, and another one right at the tip of my tongue. "You have any bacitracin, Dolores?" she asked, after she had finished examining my tongue. "I don't think she's going to need stitches, but it'd be a good idea to get some antibiotic on her chin."

"Of course we have bacitracin," Dolores answered. "This is *Rite Aid*, Violet."

"Well, go get some then," Movado the Avocado said.

Behind my teacher's back, Dolores made a face and then left the room. Olive went with her.

I looked at my teacher strangely. "You know her?"

"Shhh," she said, putting her fingers gently over my lips. "Don't talk right now. It'll makes the bleeding worse."

This situation was getting weirder by the minute. I didn't care if I bled all over the place. "No, wait a minute," I said, twisting out of her grip. "How come you're here all of a sudden? And how do you know that lady?"

Movado the Avocado sighed. "She's my sister. Last week, when we went to the craft show, I told her about you and how you're painting my room this summer. So when you came back with your *contraband*"—she paused here to raise an eyebrow—"and told her your name, she called me."

"You mean, instead of the police?" My brain was swimming around a mile a minute. "She called you?"

Movado the Avocado nodded.

"Holy cow." It was beginning to sink in, slowly. I was not going to be arrested. I would not be going to juvie. "Oh my gosh."

"Now." Movado the Avocado put her hand on my knee.

"Do you want to tell me what got into you? Why you came in here and decided to steal things? You know if you ever needed something like a toothbrush, May—"

I shook my head. "I didn't need anything. I just . . . I don't know. All these . . . things happened one after the other, and I just . . . felt so . . . sad. And I came in here—not to steal anything, honest, just to come in—and the sad feeling wouldn't go away, and then . . . I don't know, whenever that happens, when the sad feelings don't leave, I get really angry, and . . . I just started taking things." I looked down at the floor. "It doesn't make any sense," I said. "I don't even understand it, really."

"Can you tell me what you were really sad about?" Movado the Avocado asked.

I looked at my teacher. Like, really looked at her, maybe for the first time ever. I couldn't see the person I had hated all this year, the one with the big mouth and the sneering lips. Instead I saw someone who reminded me a lot of me. Someone who'd lost part of herself all those years ago when she lost her friend. Maybe someone who was still lost in a way. I didn't know.

"I was just so sad that Momma shut you out too," I said. Movado the Avocado swallowed. She put her hand over mine. "Why didn't you just tell me that Momma was Supercali?" I asked. "Right from the beginning?"

"I didn't know I wouldn't," she said. "Honestly, I didn't know what I was going to do with you this summer, May. All I knew was that after watching you struggle to keep your head above water all year, I wanted to try again, the way I should have tried again with your mother."

I hugged Movado the Avocado when she said that, overwhelmed with something I could not name. "It wasn't your fault that she got hurt," I said. My voice, which was still over her shoulder, echoed throughout the tiny room.

"And it wasn't your fault, May, that she decided to do what she did," my teacher said.

I pulled back. Shook my head. "No. I said terrible things to her that night. Things I should never have said. Things that hurt her. Right after that, she . . ."

"Listen to me," Movado the Avocado said, tilting my chin up so that I could look straight at her. Her voice was fierce. "You needed her. You deserved to have your mother present. To pay attention to you. She couldn't do that, May. She was sick because of the pain she was always in. Depressed, because of the dreams she had lost. But those things weren't your fault. They weren't even your mother's fault. It was just the way it was. It's the way things turned out. You have to stop blaming yourself, May."

I gazed at Movado the Avocado for a long moment. "I don't know how," I said finally.

Her eyes filled with tears. "I'm not there yet either," she said. "But maybe we can figure it out together."

"Maybe." I nodded.

Smiled a little.

Squeezed back when she squeezed my hand.

I still didn't know if I believed her.

But maybe, just maybe, it was a start.

48

By the time Olive and I walked back from Rite Aid, it was getting dark. Emptied of light, the bowl of sky above us had filled back up into a purplish black. A crescent moon drifted lazily to the right, and a few stars perforated the clouds. For a few blocks, the only sound was the heavy *clopclop* of Olive's new Doc Martens against the pavement. Talking right now didn't seem necessary. Plus, I wasn't sure I had the energy.

Dad's truck was parked in front of our building as we walked down Ransom Street. I sighed. There was no telling what he would have done if he'd gotten a call tonight from the Sudbury Police Department about me. I was glad he didn't have to. He'd been through enough. Thank goodness he was back. Deep down, I knew he would return.

I had some things I needed to say to him, not the first of which was an apology.

"You'll be okay up there?" Olive asked, as we paused to say good-bye.

"Yeah. We'll work it out."

"I'm glad we went down," she said. "To Rite Aid, I mean. It was the right thing to do."

"Yeah. Jeez, I still can't believe it all worked out the way it did."

"Sometimes when you take the leap," Olive said, "the net appears."

"Yeah." I looked at her steadily. "What net?"

Olive laughed. "Don't worry about it."

"No," I said, thinking about it for a minute. "I think I know what you mean." And in a weird way, I thought I might. I had taken kind of a leap, without knowing what was going to happen. And something had caught me. Something I hadn't known would be there until I jumped.

Olive giggled again. "Those two don't look anything alike! I still can't believe it!"

"You mean Dolores and Movado?" I asked.

"Yes! I never would've guessed in a million years that they were sisters."

"Movado told me about her once. She said they were really different."

"Well, I'm just glad it's over." Olive gave me a little punch in the arm. "And what'd I tell you about projecting? Totally useless, right?"

I grinned. "You were right."

"I gotta go," she said. "Text me later, okay? Tell me how things are."

"Okay." I gave her a hug. "Bye, Olive." She hugged me back quickly, but I held on a little, as if I might not want to let go. "Thanks for everything," I said over her shoulder. "I couldn't have done it without you."

Olive squeezed me back. "And you won't ever have to," she said. "Not as long as I'm here."

Dad was in the shower when I got upstairs. A large white Wendy's bag had been placed in the middle of the table, along with extra ketchup packets and two blue Gatorades. I walked past it and knocked on Gram's door.

"Gram?"

She was sitting on the edge of her bed, dressed in a pair of soft blue pants and a white shirt. Her hair had been brushed a little. The purple housecoat was draped over the back of her desk chair.

"Gram?" I said again.

She turned around, a wad of tissues clutched in one hand. Her blue eyes were swollen, but dry. "May."

I took a step forward.

She rose a little on unsteady feet. Held out her arms.

I made my way into them soundlessly, a fluid rush of movement, and as Gram's arms folded around me, it felt as if I had been holding my breath my entire life, and now I could breathe for the first time.

I closed my eyes. My voice was weak, wobbly. "I need you, Gram. When you shut the door and sleep all day, I feel invisible. I need you to be here for me."

She stroked my hair. "I know."

Somehow, despite the knot inside my chest, my voice was getting stronger. "I miss Momma too, Gram. I miss her so much. I don't know how to fix it."

She led me over to the bed and sat down next to me on the edge of the mattress. "I've been lying in here all these months thinking the same thing," she said, entwining her fingers with mine. "I'm her mother, May. I should've been able to help her. But it wasn't until you pointed things out that I finally realized something." Gram took a deep, shaky breath. "We can't fix it, May. Your mother . . . my daughter . . . made a choice that is unfixable. Nothing that we do—or don't do—will bring her back."

I began to cry then as Gram's words settled along my shoulders and crept up my neck. Sometimes missing

Momma was worse than a physical pain; it was like being eaten up from the inside out. Crying helped, I realized. A little.

Gram let me cry for a bit. She squeezed my fingers and patted my arm. Then she said, "But we can do something else, May. For Momma."

I pulled away a little. "What?"

"Forgive her." Gram cupped both sides of my face with her soft hands. "We have to forgive her. All these months I've felt completely frozen inside. But deep down, May, I was furious with your mother. *Furious.* And it scared me, feeling like that. So I just sort of shut down instead. It wasn't until you told me that you were hurting too that I realized I had to find a way out of this . . . thing . . . I had gotten stuck inside."

"I've been pretty angry too," I said.

Gram nodded. "You have a right to be. We all do. But we can't get stuck there, May. Inside all that anger. It'll eat us up. We've got to figure out a way through it." She sighed, ran her hand down the sides of my hair. "You know, the good news is that we still have what's left."

"What's left?" I repeated. "What do you mean?"

"Us," Gram answered. "We can't do a thing about Momma, May. But we can sure do something about us.

Just because she isn't here anymore doesn't mean that we're any less of a family. It just means that we've moved into a different territory. It's a whole new playing field now. And it's up to us—all three of us—to figure out what the rules are."

"That's probably the most sensible thing I've heard in a long time." Dad was standing in Gram's doorway. His hair was wet and his face had been freshly shaved. He had on a pair of clean jeans and a T-shirt.

I ran to him. "I'm so sorry, Dad. For what I said. For everything I've put you through. I just want it to be okay again with us. Please."

Dad held me tight. "Me too, May." His voice quavered a little around the edges. "I've been hard on you. Too hard." He squeezed me close. "It's been a really rough year, hasn't it?"

I nodded against the soft fabric of his shirt. "Yes." My voice was breaking.

"Can one of our first rules be that we stop yelling at each other?" Gram asked. "All of us?"

"And keep our doors open," I said. "Me included."

"I like the sound of both of those," Dad said, resting his hand on my shoulder. It was warm and soft, a perfect weight against my collarbone, like a little lopsided heart.

49

Gram's hands gripped the steering wheel of her old car as she pulled it into the parking lot and turned off the engine. We were the first ones there. I knew we would be, since Gram had said she wanted to get there early. Except for the pinchy way she was holding her mouth—which she always did when she was nervous—she looked great. Dressed in slacks, a cream-colored summer sweater, and a silk scarf around her neck, she looked like the Gram I'd always known. Maybe even better.

Now she fiddled with the knot in her scarf, untying the loose ends and shaking them out.

"Are you nervous?" I asked.

She angled the rearview mirror, checking it as her

fingers made two wide loops out of the scarf. "A little," she said, tying the loops into a bow.

I shook my head. "It looked better the other way."

Gram looked at me, exasperated.

"It did!"

She yanked at the knot, loosening it once more.

"Why are you nervous?" I asked, although I already knew the answer to this question. I was a little nervous myself.

"It's been a long time," Gram answered. "And I want to make things right."

I nodded, wondering if Olive had gotten ahold of Gram secretly and given her the life-coach speech.

"You will," I assured her.

A car pulled into the space next to us.

Gram looked over, past me and through my window. "Goodness." Her hand fluttered to her throat. "That's her, isn't it?"

The shiny blue door opened and Movado the Avocado stepped out. She was dressed in a pale yellow dress that swung lightly around her calves, a matching bolero jacket, and small-heeled, tan shoes. She raised her eyebrows when she saw me and pressed a tissue against her upper lip.

"Wow," I said. "Yeah, that is her."

Gram took a deep breath and got out of her side of the

car. "Violet . . . ," I heard her say, as Movado the Avocado came around to meet her. They stood facing each other for a moment, just sort of regarding each other, until I saw my teacher point to a bench on the other side of the parking lot. Slowly they walked over to the bench and sat down. Movado the Avocado seemed to be talking. I could see Gram fiddling with her scarf as she listened, and then nodding her head.

They sat there for at least twenty minutes, my teacher and my grandmother, talking about whatever it was they talked about. I'm pretty sure it had something to do with Momma. Most likely, they opened up that terrible time when she had had that accident on the cliffs. Maybe Gram even said something about blaming Movado the Avocado—for the accident, and maybe even for Momma's resulting depression.

Honestly, though, I'll never know what they really said. And it doesn't matter. What matters is that when all was said and done, Gram reached out and hugged Movado the Avocado the same way she'd hugged me that night. And sitting there in the front seat of her old brown car, watching her, it felt finally as if the last piece that had been missing inside the puzzle of my heart had somehow found its way back and slipped into place.

50

About twenty minutes later, Olive pulled up on her bike, even though she was dressed in her Doc Martens and a big skirt that flapped all over the place. Dad came a few minutes after that in his red truck. He looked so handsome in his pressed dress pants and oxford shirt. His harmonica was sticking out of the back pocket, and he had real shoes on.

Dad took my hand, and we led everyone along the narrow paved pathway behind the parking lot. The only sound was the *clickclick* of Movado the Avocado's heels, and the *clompclomp* of Olive's Doc Martens. Ahead of us, the tiny expanse of land was dotted with slender birch trees. Their coin-size leaves shivered in the summer breeze and made a tinkling sound above us. We continued around a bend, and then up a slight hill. And finally, three spaces over to the right, we gathered around Momma.

Her headstone was exactly as I remembered: small and flat with sharp angles. My eyes passed over the words carved in the front:

Elizabeth O'Toole
Wife,
Mother,
Daughter,
Beloved Friend
1964–2008

The last time I had been here, staring down at this stone, I had been filled with rage. The kind of rage I felt when Movado the Avocado humiliated me in front of everyone, and when Olive told me I was feeling sorry for myself, and again, when Dad admitted that he was the one behind all the work I had to do this summer.

But bigger.

It was a rage against myself, for not doing enough to help my mother, and for doing too much when I should have stepped back. It was a rage against Momma for despairing when her dream deferred had finally exploded, and for choosing to leave me behind. It was a rage I understood now, that I didn't want to make room for in my life any longer. It was something that I wanted to let go of. Replace with something else, something better.

"Good-bye, Momma," I whispered. "I love you. And I forgive you."

Dad squeezed my hand. "Good-bye, Elizabeth." His voice was choking. "I love you. And I forgive you."

Gram stepped forward and put a hand on Dad's and my shoulders. "Good-bye, my baby girl," she said. Her voice was steady. "I love you. And I forgive you."

We joined hands then, all of us—Gram, Dad, me, Olive, Movado the Avocado—around Momma, in one big circle.

We stayed there for a long time, not talking, as the birds swooped in wide arcs overhead and the trees bent their slender frames under the wind.

Then, afterward, we went home.

Gram had breakfast waiting.